As Far As
The Eye Can See

Matt Bircher

ISBN-13: 978-0-578-59895-6

Cover designed by Stephanie W. Dicken
Formatting by Polgarus Studio

For all of my family
Each of you have always been my inspiration

Acknowledgments

This new journey would not have been possible without the love and support from so many great people. First and foremost, I want to thank God for everything he has done in my life and for the many blessings that are evident every single day. I thank my amazing mother, Emma Bircher, for so many things that she does on a daily basis and for being a great help to my book. To my dad, Scott Bircher, thank you for your amazing guidance, countless support and for being my hero. My sister Maggie, thank you for inspiring me by being one of the most unique and gifted people that I know. To my grandparents, Joe and Linda Thomas, thank you so much for everything you have done by supporting me in so many ways. Also, a special shout out to Linda Thomas, "Meme", I thank you for making the quality of this book better than I could have imagined with your amazing revision. My grandparents, Jack and Julia Bircher, I thank you for your constant love and positivity. I am grateful for you guys giving me the chance to experience and learn about what was the biggest inspiration for this book. I want to thank my uncle, Scott Thomas, for being another one of my biggest influencers and role models. Also to Joey Jones, thank you for your advice and direction through this new experience. To my many other family members and friends, thank you for your endless amounts of love, encouragement, and for always believing in me.

Prologue

There comes a time in all of our lives where we look in the mirror and ask ourselves, *"Who am I?"* More times than not, we are not satisfied with the answer we get from that question. Why is that? In many cases it is because we do not know how to look at ourselves beyond the surface. Our vision is limited to only seeing what is right there in front of us. There comes a time when we have to look past the temporary things and focus on what lasts forever. Knowing who we are starts with knowing from where we come. Knowing this isn't always presented to us, we have to look for it.

This pursuit is simply a journey. A journey where it can be easy to lose yourself. With all the temporary pleasures that we face, it's easy to rely on them for fulfilment. It's not long before those temporary things disappear and, all of a sudden, we are left with a hole that only one thing can fill. That one thing is something that no job nor possession could ever come close to matching. That one thing is love. Without love in this world we live in, it is easy to become broken.

The search is not only for love but also for the people with whom to share that love. Not everyone is reared in a loving environment, and it is up to every person to find and create for themselves. When people grow up not receiving real love, there is no way they will be able to truly show it to others. It is only when a person actually receives genuine love from somebody that they can truly know it. They are the ones who will go to the ends of the earth just to get a hint of that. They are also the ones who appreciate and hold onto that feeling once they have it, and they never take it for granted.

Introduction

The campaign was over. He was lying in bed staring into space as the rain was falling on that cold November night. Lying flat on his back, he felt numb. After the party was over, the smell of champagne had faded; but there was still that same feeling of nothingness. Indeed, there was victory; but at the same time, it was all over for him. All he had dreamed of and worked so hard to achieve had been accomplished. Trying to live up to the family expectations, his whole life had revolved around this moment. Getting there at twenty-six years of age, he wondered what was left for him.

That question loomed heavy in his mind as, in the silence of his dark apartment, his eyes began to grow weary. In the past few months. he had met many smiling faces, shaken many hands, and delivered campaign promises that would please others only because nothing long lasting could please him. It was the temporary things that kept him moving forward in his life, but it was the questions that forever lingered that continued to haunt him. As the rain flowed down the window behind him, his eyes closed. Forgetting the thoughts that usually kept him up all through the night, he finally fell asleep. Perhaps his dreams would take him to a Neverland fantasy, a place to which his mind went only when he was sleeping. His dreams gave him the opportunity for his inner self to drift off beyond his wildest imagination; but, while he was awake …

there was never anything more than as far as the eye can see.

The Image

Beep, beep, beep, bee... His hand slapped around the nightstand a few times before hitting the alarm clock. It read *7:00 a.m.* He had slept an extra hour later than usual. That was only a mild start to making up for the many hours of sleep he had lost in recent months. As Evan sat up in bed, the morning sun light broke through the crack in the curtains in his apartment. He sat up and immediately grabbed his phone. He saw that the lock screen was filled with messages, missed calls and emails all rendering various forms of congratulations on the victory.

Still half asleep, he grabbed the TV remote and pressed the power button. The channel that automatically came on was *MSNBC,* the only thing he had watched during the hectic election season. As he stood up and felt the cold floor on his bare feet, he walked over to the window. Separating the curtains open and exposing the morning sunlight, he saw the beginning of a new day. The Raleigh skyline was picture perfect as he viewed it from the twenty-third floor of the *PNC Plaza.* After grasping the view, a peaceful feeling swept over him. He had rarely experienced that feeling in his life. It was a captivating moment until he turned around to see the mess in the room where he stood. The sun exposed the never ending number of boxes and campaign signs that he had to put away. The signs read, *"Stevenson for Senate: Building a Better Tomorrow."* The ultimate question now in his mind was how he could possibly attempt to become a public leader when he was so personally unhappy and uncertain of what his future held. Anyone who knew him would never think that doubt would capture his thoughts and control his mind.

From the outside, he was a charismatic guy with a great smile and one who always had a plan. He often thought that the traits others saw on the outside were plastered on him by his family. Those traits only camouflaged who he truly was. Each accomplishment added a new layer of pretense causing him to appear on the outside far different from what he felt deeply inside.

That day would be an overall humbling first day on his new journey. Unpacking his belongings needed to be done; but, before even thinking about getting started with it, he needed food. His stomach growled, but there was nothing even near to being edible in his apartment. He grabbed his coat and headed out in the hallway and into the elevator. The ride down seemed long. The elevator stopped for new passengers several times on the way down, but nobody seemed to even notice to him. This was something to which he had become unaccustomed. For the past year, everywhere he had gone he was the main attraction. Running for office had put him at the center of attention. Here, in the big city, he was just another man. As he exited the building from the main entrance, he felt the cool autumn breeze. It was truly a breath of fresh air to him. It made him feel refreshed and cleared his mind causing him to think that perhaps something new might be good for him. Maybe this wasn't such a bad situation. Maybe he could finally become his own man … be on his own.

With a cup of coffee in one hand and a bag of food in the other, he arrived back to his apartment. After eating his fast food breakfast, he wiped his hands and was ready to begin the job at hand. He took another look around the room. The apartment was to only be a temporary living situation. He planned to stay there while the senate was in session. It would work out well to use this apartment as a storage area for all the things he didn't have room for back home.

The room full of boxes had writing on them… *kitchen stuff, bathroom, living room,* and *personal stuff.* It was the *"personal stuff"* box that caught his eye. He didn't remember having it with him the previous day. His first thought was that his mother, not wanting it at her house anymore, must have sneaked it into his car at the last minute. He attempted to lift the box with one hand but had to give it a second try. Not wanting his back to strain, he used both hands and sat the box on the couch. His curiosity got the best of him. As he began to tear through the tape, he noticed the odor that smelled like twenty plus years in an attic. He wiped the dust off the box lid and opened it. Immediately he saw old pictures, scrapbooks, and a combination of rare items from his childhood stuffed into the box.

He wasn't one to reminisce or to allow himself deep feelings. Those kinds of feelings always left him in a state of anger and disappointment about how he had grown up. He had always been given all the resources he ever needed ... and still was for that matter. However, things could never mend the broken place that had always torn through his heart. His mother had always been very distant. Broken from the loss of her husband, she never fully recovered and never truly loved anyone again. She never mentioned his father. It was almost as if he never existed. It seemed that she resisted any thoughts of him. Maybe that was her way of avoiding pain that might overtake her if she thought of him.

Without having a father as he grew up, he had never been able to seek the true guidance of a male figure that he felt he, as a young boy, had so desperately needed. His mom's father was only there whenever he accomplished something worthwhile. Even then, he always pushed him to do something even better than before. It seemed he could never satisfy him. As Evan had grown older, he had begun to turn into another version of his grandfather. He was afraid to love and show affection. He really did not even know how to because emotions were never truly shown to him. This was one big reason that he always looked forward to the next thing. He really wanted to leave everything in the past.

Something caused an urgency in him to dig deeper in the box. Maybe it was just not wanting to put his other belongings into their new places. As he skimmed through old scrapbooks, he had flashbacks of all the high society events, cotillions, and academic achievements that were the main events around which his young life had revolved. None of that stuff was meaningful to him. It all represented pressure and position that he deeply hated ... until ... that one item appeared.

There in the bottom of the big box was a small gray metal box with a lock.

On it was printed *"Fireproof"* in red letters. He scrambled in the bottom of the box for a key to the lock. Without finding one, a feeling of urgency started to creep in. He knew he must open that box. Immediately he started to pull on the box trying to open it. He yanked and pulled; but he couldn't get it open. Looking around the room, he saw the box labeled *"Tool"* that was yet to be unpacked. He pulled open one side of the box and plundered for his hammer. Hammer in hand, he went right to work as if he was searching for a hidden treasure. There was nothing to lose.

He figured the neighbors were probably wondering about what was happening first thing on a Saturday morning that could possibly cause so much noise. Finally, the box broke loose with pieces of it spreading all around the living room floor. Documents and papers came out of the box and scattered everywhere, piling onto one another. A birth certificate, social security card, passport and other similar documents didn't seem worth all of the effort he had used to get access to them. However, as he gathered up the papers, he saw the top corner of what looked to be a photograph. It had fallen under his birth certificate. Without any hesitation, he slid the picture out, picked it up and turned it face up. The curiosity he had felt when he turned the picture over to view it changed into shock within a split second. There was the image of a young man holding a newborn baby. The young man's image looked almost exactly like the reflection of what he saw in the mirror every day. This picture had to be the hidden treasure that had been kept from him and had caused the emptiness he felt every single day. Nothing in the world could happen that would change what he was feeling now...

a feeling like he had never experienced before ... ever

Two Pieces

Silence... everything was quiet. Still... everything was still. There was noise around him, yet everything in his mind was silent. The world was moving, but everything in his vision had come to a complete standstill. Everything inside of him was on hold. He didn't know what or how to feel. Sitting in the middle of the floor with the contents of the box scattered around him, he did not know what to do with what he had found.

His first thought was to just put everything back in the box as if he had never even seen it and just go on with his life. He had rarely ever before needed to spend much time deciding on a matter. Most of the time, everything was decided for him; and he just did as he was told. This time was different. Nobody had given him instructions. He had found this himself. Now it was his choice.

He gathered up everything he had unpacked from the mystery box and put it back inside ... everything except the picture. He carefully placed it on a table near his bedroom door. He began to unpack the other boxes. Life must go on ... or so he thought. However, the image he had seen would begin to dominate his thoughts. Everything he viewed now was followed by a permanent watermark of a young man holding a newborn baby.

The next few weeks were tough for Evan. Any transition to a new place is difficult, but he had been hit with something really personal this time. Even though he was settled in, his mind was very unsettled. He began to really question himself. After moving from home and going to college, he had learned to be the social kind ... meeting new people and having a good time.

However, the late nights, parties, and women were all just temporary fixes. He had thought that lifestyle would improve his feelings about himself. He would have done almost anything to forget about the inner struggles he had always experienced.

The holidays were approaching, and he had promised to celebrate back home with family. It was Thanksgiving morning, but the last thing Evan wanted to do was drive in the holiday traffic to go home. He was not due back in Raleigh until the first week of January when he was to be sworn into office. However, he planned to return as soon as the Thanksgiving weekend was over. He didn't need to take much with him, so he quickly packed and headed out. He walked in the parking garage carrying a small suitcase in his right hand and a backpack over his left shoulder. When he approached his car, he remembered the picture. A small bit of him wanted to take it, but a loud voice in his mind kept telling him to just forget it. It was usually the louder voice echoing through his mind that helped him to determine the decisions he made. This time, however, was different. He knew what the past weeks had been like. He couldn't go any longer without gaining some sense of closure. He just couldn't put this feeling aside. It was much too powerful. He had to take the picture with him.

With the picture crammed in his coat pocket, he started the miserable drive down Interstate-40. The emotional numbness he usually felt slowly turned into pain. The car seemed silent. Even though the radio was playing, there was complete silence in his mind. Two hours of silence can drive any human being mad, yet it wasn't the silence that was bothering him. It wasn't even the picture. It was the question whether to push everything to which he could grow close out of the way. It was all finally catching up with him. Was it his father's fault? Could it have been a trait that has been passed down genetically?

The fuel light was a welcome excuse to break out of the silent madness he had created in his car. He took the next exit and pulled into a little roadside gas station. The sun was beginning to set, and the chill of the Autumn evening had set in. He pumped his gas and walked into the gas station. After purchasing a snack to hold him over onto the counter, he paid and made his way back into the car.

After starting the engine, he took a look at the picture. It was more like a blank stare. In that short moment, he felt his eyes watering and a single teardrop falling from his eye onto the image. Looking into the rear-view mirror, he saw the tears flowing down his cheeks. Without thinking, he let out a loud scream. All the feelings that he had bottled up inside him were coming out. He wasn't sad. He was angry. Yes, he was angry because of something that was ruining his life … something he thought couldn't be his fault. He wished he had never seen the picture of the young man who must have been his father. The only thing he could imagine was that maybe his dad had left his mother … never returning. He wiped his eyes on his shirt sleeve and held up the tear-stained picture and stared at it momentarily. With his heart and mind still in rage, he ripped the picture in half.

Red faced and teary-eyed, he pulled out of the parking lot and back onto the road. As he merged onto the highway, he pressed heavily on the accelerator causing his car to go faster and faster. The speed he drove was a reflection of his anger as he continued down the highway; and within an hour, he was back in his hometown.

Anytime he was where he grew up, his mind flooded with memories. As he pulled into the tree lined neighborhood, with large houses and manicured lawns on all sides, he was lost in his thoughts. He recalled all the times he had made the same drive, down that same road; but this time was different for him. He knew something now that he never had known before. Now it was all beginning to make sense. His whole life had been a lie … a lie that he didn't like at all.

As he neared the driveway of his grandparents' house, where his mother also lived, the driveway was lined with cars. His head lights reflected on the houses lining the neighborhood streets as he turned into the driveway. He turned the engine off and just sat in silence for a little while. He knew it would be the last moment he would have to himself for a while.

As he walked in, he saw the large staircase that graced the foyer and the enormous chandelier that lit the room hanging from the ceiling. Before he had time to take it all in, he was greeted by the family members rushing out to meet him. It was there that the relatives all gathered for Thanksgiving dinner every year. It seemed as if everybody looked about the same as last time they gathered. Each year there was very little change. There were the same formal greetings in the foyer, the same political talk, and the same sound of forks and knives on plates when they sat down to eat. This year, however, seemed to be a little different. He noticed that he was the center of attention ... as if he had moved to another level of respect. His getting elected to office had apparently made his family more interested in him this time than they had been in prior years.

After a short while of chatting, they were all seated at the table. Evan sat there making very little conversation. He barely even touched his food. He caught himself staring off into space with a blank face. He didn't care for the high praises and remarks he was hearing. It all went in one ear and out the other. His mind was not on embracing what family members had to say. He just wanted to escape.

Working was his means of escaping and putting all his problems aside. It allowed him to focus on something other than what haunted him constantly. He practiced law at his grandfather's firm, *Stevenson Law.* As a divorce lawyer, he sat in many meetings with unhappy couples were separating and divorcing. This caused him to never want to be in that situation. Even more so, it scared him. Marriage was not important to him. He felt quite self-sufficient and didn't believe he needed a wife. He had made it so far on his own, so saw no need to change anything in that regard. In his own family, he had seen broken people caused by broken marriages. They had all tried the same means of patching their lives together ... by making money. Even without marriage and a divorce, he had found himself stuck in that same trend.

It seemed to him that dinner lasted far too long, but finally the meal was over. There was more meaningless conversation before family members began to leave. Finally, all the guests left and the house became quiet. He and his grandfather were left alone in the room. They shared a few words of small talk, but there was really nothing Evan wanted to talk about with his grandfather. Actually, everything was so predictable in their lives, what could he ask that he didn't already know the answer.

Grandfather spoke up, "So .. are you all settled in your new place?"

Evan replied, "Yes sir… I guess you could say that…" That was all that was said as his grandfather looked back at the book in his lap.

With the ripped picture in his pocket, Evan knew he had to talk about it. He felt like his thoughts were burying him alive. He was digging himself in deeper and deeper as time went by. He knew he didn't want to talk with his grandfather about it. This was a conversation that he had to have with his mother. Finally, he stood and excused himself from his grandfather's presence.

Everything he has done recently has been in hesitation and second guessing, but this time he knew what he had to do. He found his mother in the kitchen.

Without any hesitation he addressed her, "Mom, can we talk in private?"

Surprised, she responded, "Well, of course!"

With his mother leading the way, they walked to the dining room, out of ear shot of his grandfather. Evan breathed deeply and quietly asked, "Has my whole life been built on a lie?"

His mother, who seemed astounded at the question, responded, "What do you mean? Of course not!"

He thought for just a second about what he was about to do. He knew that it would change their relationship for the rest of his life. Things would never be the same, but that thought made him want to do it even more. Something needed to change.

He placed his hand in his pocket and fingered for the half of the picture of his father. He pulled it out of his pocket gently. Covering it with his hand, he slid it across the table to where his mother stood. She hesitantly picked it up and turned it over to see the image on it. It was as if the picture was a magnet for tears. Within a second of her looking at the picture, tears began to roll down her face. With her other hand over her mouth, she began quietly sobbing. She had known this moment would come eventually, but nothing could have ever prepared her for it.

Evan's voice rose, "All the questions I've had about who I am my whole life have always been unanswered."

She responded, "Look, it wasn't my choice for it to be like this!"

Anger rose in his voice, "I know! It's his! He's the reason I am the way I am. He's why my whole life is messed up!"

His mother stopped him, "No, it wasn't his choice to not be here."

A questioning look came over Evan's face. She continued, "If it was up to him he would have been here through your every step, but he's gone!"

Evan fired back, "Don't you think I know he's gone? Don't you think I have realized that in every moment of my life there's been an empty space for him. Instead it's been filled with doubt and guilt."

His mother paused, realizing they were caught in a yelling match which nobody could win. She looked at Evan and softly said, "Darling…He is gone, He is dead."

Evan, with a dumbfounded look on his face, stood in place briefly. After having time to absorb what his mother had just said, he made his way to the other side of the table where she was standing. He wrapped his arms around her and began to cry.

With his head on her shoulder, he spoke, "I'm so sorry."

She stopped him, "No, I'm the one that should be sorry, I haven't been open to you." She continued, "I can't give you all the answers, I just can't…."

This encounter was very uncomfortable for Evan. He had never trusted anyone enough to open up to them. His thoughts had always been held captive inside him. He had learned to file away the things he wondered about and not permit himself to return to those thoughts. However, he had realized lately that had been a big mistake. He had decided that would never solve anything for him but would only make life worse. Now he had asked, but he had not gotten the answers he had wanted from his mother.

"So that's it?" he continued. "I've put myself through living hell just to hear you say that you can't?"

After a few seconds of silence, his mother replied softly, "Just because I can't doesn't mean that others can't."

Evan, with confusion written all over his face, replied, "What do you mean?" She continued, "I'm not the only one who ever knew your father."

She turned quickly and left the dining room. She went into the kitchen leaving the door open behind her. Evan saw her open up her address book. She took a pen from the desk and moved it back and forth on the notebook paper to get the ink to flow. Then she wrote something on the notebook paper.

Coming back to him, she handed him the paper and said, "This is the address of your uncle. If you really want to know about your father, just go there."

Evan did not know how to react. Why would she not tell him anymore than she had? What did she mean? In that moment, he realized he carried that same trait. The trait of not fully telling people what he meant must run in the family. He felt he was looking at himself from an outside viewpoint. He mentally noted to himself, "This is really how I've been my whole life."

Filled with a guilt that all started with opening the mystery box., he had now opened up a place in his life about which he was even more unsure. He could not take any more. The air in the house had become thick. He felt like he could not breath. He just needed to get out. Without further words, he walked to the foyer, picked up his bag, and opened the door. With his bag over his shoulder, he made his way to his car. He opened the car door and stood there for a few seconds looking back at the house. He got into the car, started the engine, and again glanced up at the house. As he backed out of the driveway, he had no idea where he was going. He just knew he needed to be alone. Lately he had found himself wanting to be to himself more and more often. He felt that no one else could understand his struggles or relate to the battles he faced.

The street lights were shining brightly as he drove through the town. Every place seemed to be packed with people doing their Black Friday shopping. Escaping from the crowd, feeling even more the need to be alone, Evan pulled into the empty office complex. The sign above read *Stevenson Law*. He got out of his car and slowly walked up to the door. He unlocked it, went in and turned on the lights. An odor that smelled like a mixture of paper & coffee permeated the air. This had once been the perfect place for him to hide from the rest of the world. This had been his escape. The activities here used to always be the fix for Evan as they distracted him from his real life. Now even this atmosphere just added to the long list of things that could not bring any satisfaction to him.

He walked into his office and shut the door. He leaned back against it for a moment as his eyes scanned the walls on which hung his diplomas and certificates of achievement. It was as if they were reflections of everything of which his life consisted. He wasn't pleased with the reflection he saw. He turned around and saw a clock behind his desk. It was *12:36 a.m.*

Evan turned the lights off, sat down, and leaned his chair back. He closed his eyes. His body was weary and his mind even more so. The shackles that held him back from being free when he was awake were relaxing. The cell that kept him captive was opening as he fell asleep, but still…

he was alone

The Address

Ring, Ring, Rin- ... Evan jumped, almost falling out of his chair.

Startled by the ringing phone, he sat up and answered with a scratchy voice, "He-Hello?"

The responding voice on the phone sarcastically replied, "Yep! I knew you'd be here, you workaholic…"

Evan was confused for a moment. Clearing his head to realize where he was, he answered, "Oh, yeah! Well, I guess you could call this home for me."

Evan recognized the voice of one of the attorneys in the firm as he continued to say, "Well, I just wanted to say congratulations on your victory. I hope you have found what you're looking for." Evan, not in the mood for a conversation with one of his business partners, quickly responded, "Yep, thanks … thanks a lot." He hung up the phone and thought to himself, *"found what I'm looking for?"*

The folded notebook paper with the address on it caught his eye. He had laid it on his desk the night before. He knew that today he needed to get clarity. He was going to have the opportunity to meet someone from his father's side of the family … someone who was a part of who he was.

That thought immediately inspired Evan to stand up from his chair. He looked at the clock…*8:38 a.m.* He realized that he had slept, right there in the office chair, longer than he had slept anywhere in a very long time. His neck and back felt a little stiff. He stretched out and smelled the aroma of fresh coffee. He looked at himself in the mirror, tucked in his shirttail, and fingered his hair in place.

As soon as he opened his door and walked out, a co-worker spoke to him, "Good morning Mr. Stevenson!"

She had no idea that he had slept at his desk and had just awoken about five minutes earlier. He thought to himself, *"Is this what my life has become? I'm twenty-six years old, and they're calling me Mr."* All the office employees were friends. This created a good work environment for everybody employed at the firm. As for Evan, he didn't really have many friends, not even at work. He felt it might be even harder to be friends with everyone since they were adding "Mr." in front of his last name. Even though he was the boss, he felt as if his employees were superior to him. It seemed like they had their lives all figured out. They were happy. He hadn't been able to achieve that yet. He walked over beside the front desk to pour a cup of coffee.

His secretary saw him and said, "I see you've gotten an early start this morning."

He replied, "Well, I guess I have".

The law firm kept strict business hours. They were off for Thanksgiving. In a few weeks, Christmas would be there. The minute those holidays were complete, it was back to work. Those were the two most uncomfortable days of the year for Evan and his grandfather. The office environment allowed them to operate in "business' mode which was much more comfortable for Evan than their home life. It was all starting to get the best of him ... the thought of this being his whole life. He knew it wouldn't be much better in Raleigh. It would just be a different setting with different people, but he would be the same confused man. He was ready to get going. He had a lot of ground to cover.

Speaking to a couple in the office, he said, "Well, I'm off to a meeting."

One of them jokingly replied, "I didn't know any other place was open for business today except us!"

Evan put on a fake smile and bid them goodbye.

He walked out the main entrance where the morning sun was blinding. He reached into his pocket for his Ray Ban sunglasses and put them on. He tossed his bag into the back seat and took out his phone to enter the address which was on the paper. As soon as he entered it, *"37 Minute Drive"* showed up on the screen. He was surprised to see that all this time he had been within an hour of a part of him that he had yet to discover. He would have gone any distance, paid any price, or gone to any destination. This meant everything to Evan.

During the entire drive, Evan's mind seemed to churn. He was thinking. Thinking of what to say, he tried to script words together and decide what questions to ask. He realized that he would be a total stranger to them. Why would his mother have secluded him from this part of his family? She had kept him from a big part of who he was. In his mind, there was no explanation for it. He was a smart guy.

When it came to business and politics, Evan could think outside of the box. That was a key part to his success. Up to this point in his personal life, he had never questioned the way things were. He grew up seeing that the ideal family was much different than his. He thought about all the fathers he had seen at sporting events and award ceremonies. He never had that. Evan had never questioned it until now. He just couldn't understand. He couldn't help that his father died, but how did he die? He couldn't help that his mother kept him away from his father's family, but why did she?

It was a straight drive down NC Highway 43. As he got farther from his office, he began to feel more and more nervous. It was like the decreasing minutes remaining were leading to a ticking time bomb about to go off. He felt as if he was making his way out of the hole he had been in as long as he could remember. He was pushing through, not stopping until he saw the light. The thought of that light made him anxious. He knew it would finally show who he truly was after being in dark for so long.

Everything up to this point came easy to him. School, work, anything he did … he was effortlessly good at it. He was now approaching something way bigger than himself. It was more than he could imagine. It didn't have to be this way. He didn't have to do this. He had a good career and a new venture waiting for him in the NC Senate that he had yet to start. He had an eight figure inheritance waiting for him. Deep down, though, he knew that if he didn't approach this issue, none of the possessions would mean anything to him. Knowing who he was and where he came from outweighed everything else. He had gotten himself into this. It was his choice to pursue the matter.

Just ahead he saw a sign to his right that that read "*Welcome to Vanceboro.*" He felt like he was in the middle of nowhere. He entered the small town and took at his surroundings. Evan noticed that the little town brought a sense of home to him. The small stores and shops he much preferred over the big city malls. There was just something special about it. With a speed limit of twenty-five miles per hour, he was slowed down and had plenty of time to take it all in. That was exactly what he needed. The life he had lived felt like an expressway. He was always going straight ahead at a high pace. He was never taught to take time in life to slow down and see the little things, to grasp a view of the things so many easily miss. The big picture of life had become his only view even though he knew that it was the little details that make the picture complete.

He continued on the country roads. His destination was just ahead. He pulled onto a dirt road with a sign that read *Ralph Lane.* As he slowly drove on the gravel road, he looked for 1450 on a mailbox. Not far ahead he saw a small brick house. There was a car parked close to the house and a dog lying on the front porch. This was the address that his mother had written on the paper. He pulled his car near the parked car. As he removed his glasses, he opened his car door. He felt as nervous as if he was picking up a prom date. The dog was suspicious of him and began to bark. Evan cautiously made his way up the porch steps. As he put his hand out and began to pet the dog, it calmed down. Not knowing his uncle's name, he turned around and glanced at the mailbox. He saw the last name *Miller* written on it.

He reached his hand out to ring the doorbell; but before he could do so, the wooden door quickly opened. The glass storm door remained closed. A lady wearing a nightgown and with her hair pulled up stood there.

Before Evan could say a word, she asked, "Can I help you, sir?"

Taken by surprise, he replied, "Um … Yes, Ma'am, I'm looking for your husband, Mr. Miller." With a confused look on her face, she placed her hands on her hips and said, "Very funny, Young Man! Who are you, and what are you really here for?"

Evan, confused and not knowing what he had said wrong, knew he had to say something quick before being forced to leave.

He spoke up, "I believe your husband is the brother of my late father, Edward. He's been dead for twenty-five years."

The lady at the door stared at him. She saw it. His eyes, his hair, even his voice resembled the man she once knew as her brother-in-law.

With a shocked look on her face, she whispered under her breath, "Ed…" After she gained her composure, she said, "You don't know, do you?"

He responded, "Know what?" With sadness beginning to overtake her, she had no idea how she should word what she was about to say.

"Honey," she said, "my husband and your father died at the same time."

In disbelief, Evan responded, "What?"

She opened the glass door and said, "Come on in."

Evan slowly entered the dark house. Confusion and disappointment washed over him.

The lady hurriedly excused herself saying, "I'll be right back."

Evan stood looked around the living room. There were several pictures on the walls. A large one of the lady and two young girls was hung above the fireplace. He noticed there was no father in the picture. The lady soon returned dressed differently. She noticed that he was looking at the picture.

She answered the question that was in his mind, "That is Anna and Amanda, my two daughters. That would make them your cousins."

A strong sensation came over Evan. He had never had any first cousins growing up since his mother was an only child.

Her voice interrupted his thoughts as she showed him to the couch saying, "Here, sit down."

He made his way over and sat down. "I don't believe I got your name," she said.

He quietly replied, "Evan…my name is Evan."

"Evan," she said, "There's no easy way to hear what I'm going to say, and there's no easy way to say it." He nodded his head.

She continued, "It was a wreck, a horrible car accident. It killed 'em both."

He didn't ask any more questions. He didn't want to know anything else about it right then. He was heartbroken. He knew his father was dead, but it seemed the pain became more real when she told him how he died.

On a table beside where the lady sat was a picture lying face down. She picked it up and said,

"This is him." It was a picture of her and her husband. "This is Tom and me," she said, "and this is kept in my nightstand drawer. I can't bear to see it but so often." She paused and said, "I couldn't even keep his last name anymore."

Evan had a million questions, but he didn't want to bring up anything else about her husband. He felt overwhelming sympathy ... not just for her, but for his mother as well. After all those years, without hearing a single story, seeing a face or even knowing the name of his father, he was gaining a sense of clarity. Maybe it was just too hard for his mother to talk about it. Maybe she didn't want to take him down a road full of pain that he couldn't escape.

It was quiet. An awkward silence spread throughout the living room.

Breaking it, Evan asked, "So what about your daughters?"

With her head still down, she replied, "Oh, they live far off." She continued, "They just left here yesterday. It was one of the two days I see 'em every year."

He began to feel even deeper sadness for her. In some ways he could relate to her emotions. Before he could say anything, she said, "Look, I know you're let down. You weren't looking for me."

Evan quickly responded, "But I found you, and you've helped me in more ways that you can imagine. Thank you."

As he began to rise from the sofa, she softly said, "There is one more way I might could help you."

With a spark of hope rising, his eyes turned back toward her.

She stood up and continued, "The boys grew up in a small town a little way from here. Their ancestors lived there forever. It's called *Maybree*.

After writing the name of the town on his notepad, he immediately stood up and embraced her. She gained a sense of comfort from him that she had not gotten from anyone since her husband died. It was as if he had known her for years. He usually didn't hug complete strangers, but it was desperately needed in that time. It was a connection that gave them each the motivation they needed to keep moving forward.

As he reached the door knob, he said, "I don't believe I got your name."

She replied with a soft smile "It's Cynthia."

With a smile coming to his lips, he said, "It was nice to meet you… Aunt Cynthia."

She had never heard this before from anybody. She returned his smile with the biggest smile she had smiled in twenty-five years.

As Evan opened the door, the chilly late morning air contrasted with the warm house. He walked through the front door and bent down to pet the dog. He moved with purpose as he got into his car and started the engine. As he put it into reverse, he waved to her and got another look at the house. What he thought was his final destination was only the beginning …

he must continue on

A World Unknown

As Evan pulled out of Ralph Lane, the gas light came on once again. This was a reminder of how far he had come. He hoped to find some form of gas station wherever this Maybree place was. His mood during this drive was different. The small spark of hope outweighed the prior disappointment. He had envisioned meeting a man there with slight gray hair, shaking his hand, and being able to recognize him as uncle.

He had wanted to say that to his widowed aunt, but he realized she was much too sensitive to say that to her. Now he was even more desperate for more answers … answers as simple as what his father's last name was. He was now headed to this unknown place with low gas and a sense of ambition that was greater than anything else he had every felt.

Entering in Maybree, he felt much less of a homey and welcome feel. His first view was of a run-down welcome sign and several buildings that looked like they hadn't been touched in years. There was a single stoplight, a town hall, and just what Evan needed the most… a gas station. He realized that must be his first stop before thinking about anything else. He crossed the railroad tracks, turned right down a straight road and pulled in by the *Maybree Mini Mart* sign. It was almost lunch time, and there were several trucks parked in the parking lot. There were only two pumps, and one was available. As he pulled in, he could see that his fairly new Mustang had caught the eye of the men standing around. They rarely saw anything other than a pickup truck in that area.

Evan got out of the car and smelled a strong stench in the air. It likely came from the *"Pig Palace"* which appeared to be a hog farm located across the street. He felt as if he was truly off the grid. Never in a million years would he have pictured himself in this environment. He knew he was making progress though, not just with his journey but with himself. He knew he was growing and his vision was expanding beyond the life he had lived to this point in time. Evan had finally found something he himself cared for, not something other people wanted him to do.

His stomach growled. He finally felt hungry after barely eating for the past two days. After filling his gas tank, he parked in a parking space and walked up to the store in hopes of getting somewhat of a meal. Sitting on benches in front of the entrance was a group of older men. They were talking, reading the newspaper and looking as if they didn't have a worry in the world. As Evan opened the door, an old brass bell over the door jingled. He walked in and greeted the man behind the front counter.

In the back was another counter where a full menu was displayed on the wall above it. This immediately caught his eye, and he made his way back. The tables in the back were almost completely filled with men who looked as if they were on break from a day's work outside. In his button down polo shirt and khaki pants, he looked a lot different from the rest of them. He was wearing the same outfit he had been wearing for nearly two days.

Above the counter, a sign read *Special of the Day: BBQ Chicken with Green Beans.* There was nobody behind the counter, so he rang the service bell that was on the table. As he rang it, the man who was at the front counter hurried back, and put on an apron.

The man asked, "How can I help you?"

Evan replied "I'd like the special of the day with a sweet tea."

While the man reached for a paper plate and began piling the food on it, Evan asked, "So it's just you around here working?"

The man replied, "Yep, pretty much. You looking for a job."

Evan quickly responded, "Oh no. I'm just here on business."

The worker took a look at him, chuckled and said, "Son, there's not much business to be done around here in that outfit."

The worker calculated the cost of Evan's meal … *$6.86.* Evan reached for his wallet and didn't have anything less than a twenty-dollar bill. He handed it to the worker and told him to keep the change.

Before the man behind the counter could say anything, Evan picked up his plate and drink and went to the lone empty table. Soon the men at the other tables got up, threw away their empty cups and plates, and made their way toward the exit. There he was sitting in a Mini Mart in a strange little town. Evan began to wonder, "If someone had told me a month ago I'd be here, I would've laughed." He knew it wouldn't make sense to most people, but the only thing that mattered right now was the meal in front of him and his car outside that was filled with gas.

Soon the brass bell over the door rang again. The group of men who were on their way out crowded around the man who had just walked in.

They had a brief conversation before the worker behind the counter greeted the man, "Afternoon, Mr. Linwood."

Evan looked up from his meal and saw an older man wearing a hat. His work shirt appeared a little dirty.

Linwood Johnson was a well-known man in this town. He ran a successful dairy farm. He had lived in Maybree his entire life. He was 77 years old and never went anywhere that he didn't see someone he knew. With a friendly smile on his face, he walked over to the counter. He removed his hat as he began to browse the menu.

The worker asked him, "What's it for today Mr. Johnson?"

With his hands on his stomach and then on to his hips, he replied "The special of the day is lookin' mighty good."

He exchanged his money for the plate and made his way to one of the empty tables. As he turned, Evan saw him look his way. What Evan didn't know is that Mr. Johnson noticed that he looked very familiar, almost identical to someone he had known before. Mr. Johnson looked until it almost became a stare as he then continued to the table.

He placed his hat on the table as he sat down. The table was one over from Evan, and he was on the opposite side. As he began to tear the plastic from his fork and knife, he looked over at Evan again. This time he spoke to him. Evan, with a mouth full of food, responded with a simple wave. They both ate their meals without further conversation.

It wasn't until Mr. Johnson wiped his mouth and hands and put his napkin down that he asked, "So are you from this area?"

Evan, this time, responded with, "No sir, I'm here looking for some family."

Linwood's eyes widened for a second, and then he replied, "Looking? What do you mean?"

Evan replied, "Well it's a really long and complicated story, and somehow it's led me here."

The man nodded his head and in response said, "Well, if anything is worth looking for, it's family. I hope you find whatever has brought you all the way here."

Evan needed to hear that. It encouraged him to know he was in a place where complete strangers could give empowering advice.

With a soft smile he responded, "I really appreciate it."

He took a sip of his drink and then reached his hand out to the man and said, "My name is Evan. It's nice to meet you."

The older man shook Evan's hand and, with a smile, he said, "Linwood Johnson … It's a pleasure to meet you."

After the firm handshake and noticing how rough Linwood's hands were, Evan got up from his seat. In Linwood's mind, this young man looked much too familiar; and he knew there was a good chance he'd never see him again if he left.

Linwood spoke up, "Evan, what part of town are you headed to?"

Evan, held up his hands and said, "I don't even know where to start."

Linwood laughed and replied, "Well, there's not too much to this small town; but I'm happy to help you."

Evan, without question, agreed. He knew he needed all the help he could get in this desperate search. As they both walked out of the store, a group of men were still sitting outside of the front entrance. They, of course, knew the man with whom Evan was walking. They asked him about farming, a subject that was foreign to Evan. He awkwardly stood there waiting for Mr. Johnson to finish talking.

Linwood, looking toward Evan, told the men, "Well, I better get going."

As they walked toward his car, Evan asked, "So Mr. Johnson, you know all about this area?" Linwood answered, "I'd say so, after seventy-seven years of being here." He then continued, "Why don't you just follow me…"

Without further discussion, Linwood walked over to his old Ford pickup truck, got in, started the motor and began to back out. He waited for Evan to follow him.

As Evan drove up behind the truck, they turned right onto the road. He began to have second thoughts wondering if he could really trust this man. Mr. Johnson, after all, was a stranger that he had just happened to meet a few minutes ago. He quickly dismissed that thought as he decided he had a desperate situation which called for desperate measures. He would follow anything or anybody who could help him.

As he followed Mr. Johnson, he passed through the area he had seen before as he first came into the area …the old run-down buildings and the single stop light. It was at that light where they turned left and passed over the railroad tracks. Soon after turning, there was a sign that read, *Leaving the Town of Maybree. Come Again Soon.* Now he was officially in the middle of nowhere … also known as "outside of Maybree"

As Evan continued to follow, he noticed how everyone who met Mr. Johnson going in the opposite direction waved at him. That seemed a strange thing to Evan. He grew up in a city where no one ever made a gesture to another driver unless they were angry at them. He also noticed that Linwood was a fairly slow driver. He could see him ahead turning his head left and right observing the farmland which was the scenery during most of the short drive.

After driving about a mile, they took a left turn and then a quick right. He noticed after turning right that the road sign read *Johnson Road.* Realizing that was the man's last name, he was impressed. As soon as they made their way onto the road, he saw why. Evan couldn't believe what he saw in front of him. It was a view that could have been painted on a canvas. The sun peeked through the clouds and was shining on the endless fields. His vision was filled with the farmland beauty as far as the eye could see. He began to feel something stir inside of him. He had never seen anything like what was in front him. He felt such a sense of peace. That was the sign to him that this was exactly where he needed to be.

After going a little farther, they came to the place where both sides of the road were fenced off pastures with many cows grazing. To his left, Evan saw a tall silo. Surrounding it were several barns and shelters. The pickup truck turned into a dirt driveway. There was a large sign on one of the barns that read *L. Johnson Dairy*.

Mr. Johnson drove the pickup truck under the carport of the farm house. As Evan pulled in and got out of the car, he looked all around. The two story house with white siding sat just off the road. The branches of a tall oak tree were peeking from behind it. Mr. Johnson got out of the truck, made his way over to where Evan was parked.

"Welcome to my farm." He said.

Evan told him how beautiful everything looked but wasted no time in asking, "So, did you need to stop here before you show me where to go?"

Mr. Johnson looked serious as he said, "Well, I think I have a few things inside that'll help."

He now had Evan's full attention, and he followed him as he began to make his way over to the side door of the house. With the door already unlocked, Linwood opened the door and walked inside with Evan right behind him. As they entered in the house, it appeared as if nothing had been touched in decades. Straight in front was a wood stove. After showing Evan to a seat in one of the chairs by the wood stove, Mr. Johnson opened the back door and went to the back porch. Evan looked around the farm house, feeling as if he had stepped back in time. Mr. Johnson came back in with an arm full of firewood logs. He placed them on the floor and opened the door of the wood stove. The hot air escaped into the room as he tossed a log in.

He then wiped the debris from his hands motioned to Evan while saying "Follow me."

Evan got up from his seat; and, once again followed as Mr. Johnson led the way. They walked through a hallway that led to a small narrow staircase.

Before going up the steps, Mr. Johnson looked back to Evan and said, "Watch your head."

Evan nodded, and they continued up to the second floor. When they reached the top of the staircase, the second level was a small space with only two doors. The old man walked over to the center area and pulled a string that hung from the ceiling to bring down the folded steps.

The steps, looking as if they could give out at any second, made squeaky noises as he eased up them.

Standing on the attic folding stairs, Mr. Johnson asked Evan, "So, who is it in specific that you're looking for?"

Evan replied, "My grandparents are supposed to have lived around here. They were my father's parents, but I never met them… or him."

Still scrambling around in the attic, Mr. Johnson asked, "You've never met your father?"

Evan replied, "Well, he died soon after I was born, and I've never known his family."

With his upper body in the attic, only the old man's legs could be seen from the Evan's view. Knowing he couldn't be seen, Mr. Johnson, filled with emotion, felt the tears forming in his eyes. He cleared his voice and called Evan closer. He handed him a bin that was heavy and covered with dust. As Evan struggled to get control of it, he didn't know how Mr. Johnson was able to pick it up with such ease. Evan, in that moment, remembered the things he had opened two days before that had led him to this place. Much like these, they hadn't been opened in years.

With the bin in his hands, Evan eased down the narrow staircase. Mr. Johnson was behind him trying to get himself together. He walked over to the chairs by the wood stove and sat the bin down onto the floor. Mr. Johnson took a seat in the chair beside Evan. He began to open a bin that was completely filled with scrapbooks.

He said, "While my wife was living, she worked on making these just about every day. I haven't looked at 'em in years."

Evan saw what he thought might be an old picture of the two of them hanging on the wall. It seemed to be the only picture in the entire house. He curiously began to wonder about her and what may have happened. Evan glanced over at the man who was flipping through the books and reminiscing with a smile on his face.

Evan then asked, "So what is it that I'm here for? What is here that can help me?

Mr. Johnson paused for a moment and said to him, "I know what you're feeling."

Evan, who thought it was impossible for anyone to do so asked, "So, what is it that I'm feeling?"

Linwood scrambled through the bin and pushed aside several books. He pulled out a folder with the words *The Boys* on the front of it. He dug around through the folder and pulled out a picture. He placed the picture in Evan's hand with it faced down. He didn't say anything

Evan turned the picture over to see a faded picture of a young man with Mr. Johnson standing beside him with his hand on his shoulder. He sat quieting looking at the images for a few moments. Then he remembered. He still had the photograph in his pocket that he had ripped in half. He pulled it out slowly, he placed the two pictures side by side. He realized it was the same man in both pictures.

He got up from the chair and walked over to a small mirror on the wall. He looked at himself and then at the picture. He looked almost identical to the young man in the picture. Mr. Johnson walked behind him and placed his hand on his shoulder. Seeing their reflection in the mirror was almost an exact duplicate of what he saw in the picture...

the puzzle was now complete.

The Missing Piece

Evan was in shock. He was experiencing so many different emotions that were still new to him. It was exactly what he had been waiting for all of this time. All the miles traveled, tears shed, and so many ups and downs had led him to where he was standing in that very moment.

"Evan Michael Stevenson," Mr. Johnson said, "born on February 10th 1993."

His face said it all. He had known all this time and had been trying to hold his emotions back ever since he ran into Evan earlier that day. The reflection in the mirror changed as Evan turned around and embraced the man like he had known him his whole life instead of just a few hours. He felt as if he was getting good at hugging strangers, but this was different. This was his own flesh and blood ... a part of who he was. He wouldn't be here if it wasn't for this man his arms were wrapped around. There had never been a time in his life when he had felt like he did at that moment. He had never pictured his life this way. He was gaining a new perspective on who he really was.

Evan looked at Mr. Johnson and asked, "How did you even have the slightest idea of who I was?"

With a smile spreading on his face, he answered, "As soon as I saw you, I saw something I hadn't seen in years."

Evan replied, "What was that?" Mr. Johnson paused for a moment and then said to him, "My family."

Knowing that his two sons were gone and that his wife had passed away, it all started to add up for Evan. He no longer saw this elderly dairy farmer as

Mr. Johnson. He now saw him as Linwood Johnson, his grandfather; and he realized that he was all his grandfather had left … and that his grandfather was all he had left of his own father.

The sympathy they felt for each other as they looked into each other's eyes was like nothing either one of them had ever experienced. Nobody but the two of them could understand the emotion that welled up inside them. Each of their lives had been lived in different ways, in different places … but with the same longing. They shared something special. It was that missing link in each of them that they both had finally found.

For twelve years, Linwood had been on his own. He had risen early in the morning to do farm chores, kept himself occupied throughout the day, and then went back to work in the late afternoon. The farm was what had kept him going. Other than the farm and church, there wasn't much else he did. Every day for fifty-five years he had pretty consistently followed the same routine at the same times every day. He never talked about his feelings to anyone. Whenever he was with other people, he would put a smile on his face to try and cover the brokenness he felt. After his sons died, his wife was all the family he had. They helped each other cope with the pain of such a tragic loss. Married for over 50 years, a diagnosis of cancer would take her away from him in less than a year.

Evan and Linwood sat in front of the wood stove and looked through an endless stack of photographs. Years of pictures of Evan's father and uncle gave him insight as to his father's early life. They were all kept in a separate folder which was set aside from all of the other pictures. Each picture revealed something new for Evan. He had only seen a single picture of his father up until this point. It was all so overwhelming. Nothing needed to be said. Everything he had wanted to know was right in front of him as if they were speaking to him. That gave him a sense of belonging to this new part of his life he had found.

This all seemed fairly new for Linwood as well. It had been years since the box full of pictures had even been touched. Evan curiously mentioned the pictures in the envelope.

He asked, "Why are these separate from the other ones?"

Linwood responded, "Well, my wife, your grandmother, took out each one from the pages of the books. She was so torn apart after losing her sons, she couldn't bear to look at them."

Not knowing how to correctly respond to that, Evan just nodded his head.

Linwood continued, "Then, after she was gone, I couldn't bear to even look at the box…it just hurt too much."

Evan began to see a trend. It seemed that everyone he encountered had stored their sadness away. It was as if they'd locked it up and left it someplace where it couldn't make them uncomfortable. He had done the same thing his entire life.

As the hours of reminiscing went by, Linwood rolled up his left shirt sleeve and looked at his watch. He noticed that it was nearing four o'clock. It was almost time to go back to work.

He said to Evan, "Well, I guess my extended lunch break is about over."

Somehow and for some reason, this seventy-seven-year old man needed to go back to doing what he had done every day for over half a century.

He and Evan got up from the chairs in front of warm wood stove and made their way into the kitchen.

At the same time, a man peaked open the side door and loudly said, "I know you ain't taking no day off, Mr. Linwood!"

He responded, "Oh, you know better than that. I'll be right out."

He slid open a door and grabbed his work boots and coveralls.

Evan asked, "Who was that?"

Linwood replied, "That's James. He's been helping me here for years. My old bones can't handle this all by myself anymore."

With his coveralls on and his boots in one hand, Linwood made his way out the side door with Evan walking behind him. Linwood sat on the bench on the porch and began to put his boots on. As he was doing that, James walked over near them. Linwood knew that he was curious about who the young man was.

Linwood said to him, "James, right here is my grandson. He stopped over to visit."

James' brow furrowed as he said to Evan, "Well then … that's news. Good to see you."

They shook hands, and James began to eye Evan from top to bottom. He noticed his polo button-down shirt and the Rolex watch on his wrist. James didn't know what to think of this guy he had just met. He walked toward the barns where he could get back to work.

Linwood slowly got up from the bench and asked Evan, "Have you ever camped or fished before?"

Evan, without having to think, replied "Can't say that I have done either one of those things."

Linwood, nodding his head, said, "Yeah, I thought so. Well, if you come back on over tomorrow, I've got a pond down the road. I need to get back up there. Would you want to join me?"

Evan, without any hesitation, said, "Of course!"

Linwood, who had a smile on his face replied, "Be back about mid-afternoon tomorrow. I'll see you then."

He put his hand out to Evan, and they firmly shook hands. Linwood then turned and walked toward his afternoon work that was awaiting him. Evan was blown away. There was no emotional embrace, just a strong man-to-man handshake.

He got into his car and sat that there for a second. He reached for his phone. He couldn't remember the last time he had gone this long without even looking at it. There were dozens of notifications on the screen, but there was one that stood out above the rest. It read, "*Mom: Missed Call (4)*" Without any hesitancy, he immediately swiped to call her. The phone rang a couple of rings and stopped.

Before she could even say anything he said, "Mom, today's been crazy. I'm coming home. I promise."

He hung up the phone. He knew everything else needed to be said in person. He hadn't spoken to her since the night before, when he had left the house with a heavy heart and deep emotions.

As Evan started driving back home, his mood was completely changed. He felt a sense of peace that he had never truly had in his life. He had finally found some clarity to his questions, but there was still more that he wanted to know. Knowing where he now could get those answers made all the difference for him.

He took in the view of the scenery from country roads as the sun was beginning to set in the late afternoon. He began to gain appreciation for simple things that had gone unnoticed in his mind before. He felt as if the things that held him back were beginning to clear and that nothing could get in his way … nothing except for a mother whom he was going to face when he arrived home.

The view changed as he left the countryside and got closer to the city. The traffic got heavier and the pace of life got quicker. When he drove back into his home neighborhood, it was dark outside just as it had been when he left it. As he drove up in the driveway, he looked at the large house. A strange feeling crept over him. It had nothing to do with how he felt about his grandparents … nothing had changed with them. It was how he was feeling about to his mother. He felt like he now better understood the way she had lived her life since her husband, his father, had been gone. They now shared a deep loss.

With his car parked in the driveway that circled the front yard, he walked up the steps. Before he could even get to it, the door swung open. It was his mother. Before she could even say a word, Evan opened his arms and embraced her. He felt like everything now made sense. He felt like he knew both sides of who he was.

His mother broke the silence when she asked him, "Where on earth have you been all this time?"

For him, the past twenty-four hours had flown. He realized it must have been different for his mother.

He replied to her, "I had to be on my own. I had to find the missing pieces that were never put together."

She had a pleased look on her face. She had never seen her son open up in any personal way to her or to anyone.

She then said to him, "Well let's find out about it over dinner."

They walked through the foyer and into the living area where his grandfather looked as if he hadn't moved since the night before.

He spoke to Evan, "Well, about time you came downstairs, boy."

He hadn't even noticed Evan had been gone. Evan gave him his best fake smile as they walked into the dining room. The table had already been set and their meal was waiting for them. Evan remembered what had happened the last time he was in this same room. He also knew that, if he had never had the courage to show his mother the photo, he wouldn't feel like he felt at that moment. In his mind, he was thinking of how much difference one day could make. With a rejuvenated spirit and attitude, he now felt there was a lot that needed to be said at the table.

"So… tell us .." His mother said as they were sitting down, "What happened?"

Not knowing where and how to start, he cleared his throat and began. "I made my way over to the address you gave me. The name *Miller* was on the mailbox, and a lady named Cynthia was there."

His mother tried to recall the name. "Miller? that last name doesn't sound familiar," she said.

"What about Tom?" Evan replied.

"What do you mean, what about him?" "Was he there to answer your questions?" she asked.

Evan replied, "Mom, he died with my father, in the same car, at the same time."

Her face turned pale, and she went into a momentary state of shock.

Evan frantically shook her and yelled, "Mom!"

Looking like she had just been awakened, she said, "Oh, sorry! Ju-Just continue."

With a look of concern on Evan's face, he resumed the conversation, "So she sent me to the area where he and my dad grew up."

Her eyes growing wide once again, she asked "and…?" She was on the edge of her seat.

Evan said, "And, I ran into a man named Linwood Johnson."

His mother immediately became more alert and appeared more interested now than ever. (The last name Johnson was automatically recognizable. It was once almost hers.)

She quickly asked, "So you talked to him?"

Evan answered, "Of course, and I'm going back over to his farm tomorrow. It's really nice over there."

"Oh, I don't know if that would be a good idea." she said.

Puzzled by her response, he asked, "What are you talking about? Why wouldn't it be?"

She replied, "I just don't want you to be hurt again. You're better off just knowing what you know now. You've found what you were looking for. Just know, it's best to just go on with your life." At this point, his grandfather spoke up and said, "Son, you've got enough in your life that's important to you. Don't spend your time on anything that will get in the way of it."

Evan began to feel very frustrated. He felt like there was no way that his family would allow one good moment to last between them. Determined not to let his frustration ruin his improved spirit, Evan mulled over in his mind what his grandfather had said. As he did, a spirit of boldness arose in him.

In a respectful but firm voice, he spoke back to his grandfather, "Important to me ... or to you?" He continued, "I know now what is important to me, and I'm not going to let the things you've wanted for my life to affect it."

He knew immediately that was not what his grandfather had expected him to say.

The conversation at dinner had all of a sudden taken a turn for the worse. Evan remembered now why conversation had always been limited when they ate together. The atmosphere became awkward, and he couldn't sit there any longer. He got up and thanked his grandmother for the meal. She was the only one he felt he could say anything to at that moment. He took his plate into the kitchen and then made his way upstairs. He truly felt like leaving the house entirely ... the same feeling he had the night before. However, this time he knew where he needed to go and where he wanted to be. To Evan, it didn't matter if his family was against it. He didn't intend to find what he had been searching for his whole life and just walk away from it. There was still so much more to know. He wondered why his mother didn't want him to know any more than what he had learned that day? Had she been hiding something all of this time? Now he couldn't help question if it was sorrow that had kept her silent for all these years...

or was she hiding some mysterious secret?

Four to Seven

In Maybree Linwood went to sleep while most people were finishing dinner. He set his clock for 4:00 a.m. He had done that for most of his life. At that point, he didn't think much about it. It had been easier for him to live by his schedule in recent years. He hadn't felt the desire to stay up later the way he had in years prior. It was just him … alone. He could escape his loneliness in his sleep and while he worked. The always knew there would be plenty to do when he woke up. It was a similar story and the exact feeling Evan experienced. For the both of them, however, this was like a new beginning causing them to feel better about the world they'd wake up to in the morning. Knowing there was someone else who understood how they felt made all the difference.

Linwood was awakened by the sound of a local AM radio station on his clock that had been on his nightstand for years. He turned his lamp on making the small picture frame with his wedding photograph in it visible. He got out of bed and slowly bent down beside his bed on his knees to pray. He began all of his days with this same routine.

He took time to grab a banana from the kitchen counter to hold him over until the morning chores were complete. He opened the back door to darkness except in the area where the farm lights lit up a portion of the yard. His right- hand man, James, had already turned them on. James had been working every day on the farm since he was a teenager. He kept the same schedule as Linwood. He was like a son to Linwood, especially after he lost two of his own. James lived in a small three-room house that was located on the farm land. He was always early and ready to get started when it came to working. As Linwood got older, James had helped to motivate him to keep going. Without each other's help, the farm couldn't operate.

Linwood ran a large dairy farm. He had inherited it from his father when he was only twenty years old. At that age, he had thought he wanted to have a change of scenery and to do something different with his life. Linwood had been in college for a year when his father became sick and was unable to work. He came back to the farm to help and from that time on had spent every morning gathering and positioning over one-hundred cows to be milked. The other half of the morning was spent feeding all of the cows. He did this two times a day. All kinds of other farm work took place during the remainder of the day. It was a busy job of hard work, and he couldn't do it alone.

As Linwood and James completed their work that morning, it was just past 7:00 a.m. The sun was rising, and most people were just getting up. The air was cold and thick throughout the morning. This usually made it difficult for Linwood to work, but he had pushed through as he always did. Finished with their morning work, they made their way back to the house. They took off their muddy and manure-covered boots and left them on the side porch. They washed their hands in the small bathroom that had been added onto the house near the back door. Then they headed to the kitchen where Linwood got the coffee machine going. He opened the refrigerator door and took out a carton of eggs. Each morning, after washing up, he and James ate breakfast together. That day was no different except for one thing.

James still hadn't mentioned Linwood's grandson whom he had met the day before. There were lots of questions looming in his mind about him. He thought, after being with him for such a long time, he would've heard about Linwood's grandson before now. He knew it needed to be discussed. Linwood put the bowl of scrambled eggs on the small table by the window where James was sitting.

James took a sip of his coffee, cleared his throat, and then asked Linwood, "So, your grandson ... he doesn't come around here much does he?"

Linwood walked back over to the table with a plate full of bacon in his hand. He put the plate on the table and sat down across from James.

He then responded, "Yesterday was the first time I had ever met him."

James wasn't too surprised. He said, "That's gotta be Ed's boy."

Linwood nodded his head and said, "Almost identical."

Their breakfast conversations had never gotten into personal family matters nor any deep subjects before. Those type things never came up. They always talked about work or sports or the weather. This conversation was different.

James put his fork to his plate of eggs and asked, "So, is he coming back?"

Linwood replied, "He should be back later today. We're supposed to be heading up to the lake."

James was a little skeptical about this plan as he was very protective of Linwood. They shared a special bond that went beyond just working together on the farm. They had been each other's form of family. When James' father was killed, Linwood and his wife had taken him in and supported him for years. They gave him a job and a place to stay and even helped him get his GED. James felt like he owed it all back to Linwood; and, as he got older, he determined it was his duty to help care for him.

"I'm not too sure about this." James said. He continued, "Why is it that now this guy all of a sudden wants to come here and find you?"

Linwood responded, "You know, I'm not really sure. Maybe the Good Lord is trying to use me to help him out with something … or maybe He's using him to help me."

James responded, "I'd have a hard time believing that fella would need help with anything after seeing what he had parked in your driveway."

Linwood let out a chuckle, then responded, "But you know, James, there's more to a happy life than material things. As for me, I could have anything in the world; but, without loved ones, things aren't worth having. I think he just needs somebody."

Linwood knew well about this. It was like he said that for himself. He had everything that he could need. With very few loved ones in his life, those possessions didn't matter. He was indeed successful, and he had done well in farming throughout his life. Recently, it was the bigger things in the picture of life that he had been longing for.

Anybody who knew Linwood didn't have any questions about him on a personal level. He was a good church-going, God-fearing man who seemed to have had lived a complete life. From the outside, there was always a smiling face at every encounter with people. The inner feelings, however, were constantly dulled by loneliness. Since dealing with such great personal loss as the untimely death of both his sons and then his wife, this was the one time he had found someone instead of losing them. He knew he couldn't question this encounter. He hadn't experienced precious moments with family in a long time. He really needed this …

but was it for the long term or just a passing fancy?

Long Roads

Evan woke up with a determination to leave all the confrontation behind him. He knew there were more important things that would take place later in the day … more important than any meeting in which he had ever participated. This was a bigger opportunity than any he had ever experienced, but there would be no financial gain involved. It was all personal gain for him … gain of a sense of understanding of the people in his life he had never known and some that he had known his entire life.

In a white T-shirt and pajama pants, Evan went downstairs and made his way into the kitchen. He found his grandfather sitting, as usual, with a newspaper in one hand and a cup of coffee in the other.

His grandfather, eyeing Evan's attire, asked, "Why aren't you dressed for work?"

Evan pulled his phone from his pocket and looked to be sure what day it was.

He responded, "What are you talking about? It's Saturday!"

His grandfather looked straight at him and grumpily said to him, "You should have thought about that when you left work for the day yesterday. Someone has to pick up for your slack when you're not there, and that someone is you."

Evan thought to himself that it was too early to be having this kind of conversation. He moved on to the kitchen and grabbed a box of cereal. He opened the cabinet to get a bowl and began to pour the cereal.

He was interrupted by another comment from his grandfather, "That little issue that was brought up at dinner won't be a problem now, will it?"

Evan replied, "If you call working through personal issues for the first time in my life a problem, then … yes, it will be."

As soon as he finished his cereal, Evan got dressed, got his things together and left for the office … not to work, but to escape. The next several hours couldn't have gone by any slower for him. The last place he wanted to be was at the office. He wasn't doing any work … he was the sitting. That was not usually the case for him. He had always prioritized making money above anything else. That was why he woke up in the mornings. Until now, there had not been anything else worthwhile to him. He now felt that everything in his life had been switched around and changed. He didn't care if he never stepped foot in that office again. He knew it was a representation of the person he had become … the person he was now trying not to be.

Just after noon, Evan heated up Ramen that he found in the break room and found himself elbow deep in a bag of chips. His feet were kicked up on the table while he watched the office television. He constantly eyed the clock … just waiting to leave. What was waiting for him was a place totally opposite of where he sat now. It was a place he wanted to be and wanted to know more about. Though life was different there, it was much better. It represented the other half of him… the better half. It had only taken one single visit there for him to understand that.

It still wasn't time to leave, but he just couldn't stay there any longer. He knew he would be early, but he couldn't stand the boredom any more. Evan got up from the office desk chair and turned off the television. He put on his coat and picked up his brief case and walked out of his office closing the door behind him. As he neared the front entrance, he turned around and looked at the office. A strange feeling came over him. It was as if he never wanted to step foot in that building again. He opened the door to be greeted by the early afternoon sun shining brightly. He locked the door behind him. Soon he was back on the road where he had spent a lot of time the past few hours. He had to stop for gas again, but this time Evan's mind was focused on the next stop he intended to make.

Things were different about the drive to Maybree that time. It seemed much quicker. His thoughts were more optimistic. There were still things he needed to know, and he knew he was relying on the best person there was to help him.

When Evan arrived back at the farm, he saw Linwood sitting on his front porch. He thought to himself, "That's my grandfather." A sense of warmth came over him … a feeling that was so foreign to him. He parked in the driveway and opened his car door. The odor in the air again hit him, but it didn't seem to smell nearly as bad as it had the day before. It simply gave proof to the environment where he was.

He grabbed his small bag and walked over to the front porch. As he neared Linwood, he saw that he was asleep in the rocking chair. He stood for a moment just watching him snooze peacefully, but he knew they had plans. He reached over and softly tapped Linwood's shoulder.

Immediately Linwood jumped and looked up at Evan. "Well you're early." he said, while checking his watch.

Evan replied, "I know. I'm sorry to interrupt your naptime, but I just couldn't stand being where I was any longer."

Linwood rose from the chair, stretched his arms above his head, and said, "Oh you aren't interrupting anything. I was just catching up on some sleep. We can get going."

He walked down the front steps on the porch with Evan behind him.

He turned to Evan and said, "I thought I was dreaming when I heard the sound of a car on this road."

After gathering a few items, they got into Linwood's old Ford pickup truck and pulled out of the driveway.

As they made their way onto Johnson Road, Linwood said to Evan, "I need to make a quick stop." Soon the truck began to slow down as Linwood drove into a narrow driveway just off the road.

"I'll be right back." Linwood said, as he opened the truck door.

He walked to the small house, gave a quick knock on the door, and opened it. As Linwood entered, James was sitting on his couch.

"What do I owe you for this visit, Mr Linwood?" James asked with a smile.

Linwood replied, "Is a day's work possible?"

James's smile suddenly faded, and a more serious look came to his face.

"I see. So I guess y'all are headed off." James said.

Linwood replied, "Understand, James, this is important. Can you get a few of the other guys to give you a hand?"

"Yeah, I guess I can rally some people together" James said.

Linwood responded, "Thanks, I really appreciate it. I'll owe you one." He made his way out the door with James following him.

James knew how far he had come because of Linwood's help, and replied, "It's my pleasure."

As Linwood walked back to his truck, James spotted Evan waiting in the passenger seat. He was still trying to figure this guy out. He knew he wouldn't be able to right away. They came from different worlds. He stood in the doorway and watched as Linwood backed out of his driveway where he and his grandson made their way back onto the road.

Linwood pulled down the sun visor as the mid afternoon sun was shining through the windshield. When they got to the end of Johnson Road, they turned onto another road which led them onto an overpass. Evan noticed from the window that all the cars on the highway below were traveling at high speeds and going in both directions. It was hard to believe that this heavy traffic would be so close to this almost forgotten little town of Maybree.

Evan spoke up, "I guess not too many people take the Maybree exit do they?"

"When you're going so fast, it's hard to slow down" Linwood replied.

Evan laughed a little to himself. He knew exactly what that meant.

A short distance from the busy highway, they turned left onto a dirt road where a yellow gate was opened. There was nothing but wooded area on both sides. The straight narrow dirt road appeared to go on forever.

Evan asked, "So how far back is this lake you're talking about?"

Linwood replied, "Well, it's a good little way back there."

As they neared the end of the straight road, the view began to widen. Straight ahead of them were endless fields as far as Evan could see. He was blown away once again. The view was like nothing he had ever seen. Linwood drove on and turned left continuing on the dirt road that edged the fields and ran parallel to the highway. The speeding cars were visible. Seeing them speed by seemed to make the old Ford truck feel like it was in slow motion … just like Evan's mind was in that moment.

Linwood slowed the truck even more as he pulled up to a cable hanging between two tree. Evan assumed this must be marking where Linwood's property started.

Linwood put the brake on the truck and asked Evan, "You mind unhooking that wire for me?

Without hesitating, Evan answered, "Of course not."

He opened the door and walked to the cable thinking to himself, "How hard can this be? Anyone could get in here." He grabbed the hook and tried to lift and pull it out. It was obvious to Linwood that he wasn't having much luck. He sat there and watched Evan struggle for a few minutes trying to unhook it. Then he slowly got out of the truck and walked over to Evan, whose hands were nearly blistered.

"I guess it's doing a pretty good job" Linwood jokingly said.

Evan had a look of total embarrassment on his face as Linwood took hold of the clip, turned it sideways, and lifted up the wire to unhook it.

He said, "It's a nice little trick I learned."

He had figured that Evan had never done anything like that before, so he allowed him to struggle just so he could teach him something.

With that explanation, Evan's embarrassment was short-lived. They soon came to a smaller road.

Linwood pointed over to the trees that lined both sides and said, "These right here are cherry trees that were planted by hand many years ago. When they bloom in the spring, it's one of the pettiest sights you'll ever see."

There was still no sign of a lake. Ahead Evan saw another opening in the trees with an even heavier chain to block it off and a sign on it that read *Private Property*.

Linwood, with a gentle smile coming to his face, looked over to Evan and said, "Don't worry, I'll take care of this one."

Evan began to laugh as Linwood made his way out of the truck. He watched him walk over to the gate and pull a key from his shirt pocket. After

45

unlocking it, Linwood drove the truck slowly on the pathway that sloped slightly upward. The leafless trees made some of the water below visible as they looped around the property.

Nearing the end of the road, Evan was surprised to see a small wooden house come into view. After just a short drive farther, Linwood parked the truck in a short driveway in front of it and turned off the engine.

Evan got out of the truck and immediately asked, "What's this?"

Linwood proudly put his hands on his hips and responded, "This is the ole cabin."

With Evan still taking it all in, Linwood walked over to the side of the cabin.

He turned to face Evan and said, "The best part is in here."

They walked up the steps, and Linwood opened the screen door and waved his hand for Evan to go in. Evan walked in the cabin with Linwood following behind him. The first thing he noticed was a screened porch overlooking the lake. The water was still, and the tree reflections looked as if they were painted onto the surface.

Linwood said to him, "You just can't beat that view."

Evan asked, "So you built this?"

Linwood replied, "Well, not just me. I did it with the help of my sons." Linwood opened up the sliding door that led to another room in the cabin and said, "We thought it'd be better than tents."

Evan felt emotional knowing that he was standing in a place that his father had helped create.

Linwood said to him, "I come up here just about every day between the morning and afternoon chores. It's so peaceful here."

The view was breathtaking. The lake below was surrounded by the fields that were beyond it. Evan felt he could gain a better sense of understanding nature looking at it from this perspective. In the corner of the cabin, there were several fishing poles.

Linwood grabbed a couple of them and said to Evan, "Let's get to it. We don't have long before the sun goes down."

They both walked down the stairs that went to a small dock out over the water. Two chairs were waiting at the end of the dock, and they both sat down. It was a relaxing moment for Evan. He had never done anything like this before. The water was still, and the only sounds came from the cars on the distant highway.

Linwood casted his line out in the water like he had done many times before.

He said to Evan, "So, you look like you're successful. What kind of work do you do?"

Evan had almost forgotten that the two were still basically strangers. That feeling was enhanced by the close connection he had made with Linwood the day before. He felt like he had known him his whole life.

Evan replied, "Well, I've worked in my family law firm for a couple of years. I just got elected as a state senator as well."

Linwood, seeming impressed, asked, "You're how old again?"

Evan responded, "I know... trust me I know."

Linwood said, "Family businesses are tough. I can say that from my own experience. I always wanted to try something else, but my father had everything planned out for me. He really wanted me to keep this farm going. After he passed away like he did, I didn't wanna let him down; and here I am fifty-five years later still doing it."

Evan found himself being able to relate to something Linwood had gone through. He didn't want to be stuck doing the same thing for all of his life. He knew he needed to find his own interests instead of working and living out someone else's dream.

The sun reflected on the water making it look like a masterpiece as it began to set. They continued to sit there. Everything was quiet except for the sound of Linwood casting his line in the water every now and then. The silence allowed nature to speak into Evan's mind some things that he had never heard before. Those things had always been blocked out by the noise of his ego and expectations.

As it began to grow darker, Linwood pulled in his line and said, "Well, I guess we better head back on up. There's not much biting tonight."

They walked back up the steep stairs and made their way into the cabin.

Evan, realizing it was nearing dinner time, asked, "Do we have to catch our dinner?"

Linwood laughed and responded, "I'm afraid not tonight." He pulled out a bag of wieners and said, "Luckily I brought these, but they're no good without a fire to cook them on."

Evan was relieved as they made their way outside to the fire pit. Linwood went over to his wood stack and chose a few pieces to start the fire.

Noticing that there was only one seat by the pit, Linwood told Evan, "You'll have to grab another seat from inside. I usually don't have a need for more than one seat out here."

When Evan came back out with the seat, the fire was roaring and smoke floated into the pitch black sky. The fire brought a warm feeling as the night grew colder. Linwood had two sticks hewn out for skewers, and he handed one to Evan. He and Linwood sat across from each other with the fire between them. As they held the wieners over the fire, Evan knew he hadn't learned much about his father and he wanted to know more.

Evan finally broke the silence. He asked, "So what can you tell me about my father?"

Linwood looked up at him and said, "How long have you been waiting to say that?"

Evan replied, "Well, it's such a fragile subject to talk about. I guess that's why I was never told anything about him when I was growing up."

Linwood was not one to discuss things like this. He did, however, understand how important it must be for Evan to learn about his father. This would be news that Evan could never have been prepared for …information he would never forget.

Before Linwood could speak, Evan told him, "I know how it all happened. Cynthia told me."

Linwood quickly said, "Cynthia? How on earth did you know to find her."

Linwood had not seen her or heard from Cynthia since his wife's funeral. Cynthia had taken care of Linwood's wife in her final years, and she was there when she passed away. He hadn't seen or heard from her since then.

Evan answered, "My mother had her address. She didn't even know your other son had passed away too." He continued, "When I told her that he was gone, she completely freaked out. Why doesn't she know anything?"

Linwood quietly said, "I think your mother knows better than anyone else…"

Except for the crackling sound of the fire burning, it became dead silent. Evan didn't know what that could mean.

After a moment of wondering, he asked, "What…What is that supposed to mean?"

Linwood knew what he would say next could change Evan's perception of his mother. He also knew it could do more harm than good. Linwood looked at Evan as he sat that there looking as if he was on the edge of his seat. His face begged him to say something … anything.

Linwood spoke slowly, "Your mother knows better than anyone because she was there when everything happened…

she was the one driving."

Lost to Found

Evan's felt his face flush. He felt anger arising in him. He thought of all the difficult times he had experienced with his emotions. His mother wanted to pretend the situation never happened. He now was able to see that not only was it her fault for never being honest, it was also her fault that it even happened. It was all starting to become clear in Evan's mind. This was why she didn't want him here with his grandfather.

Linwood saw Evan's raw emotions from the look on his face and his heavy breathing. He knew there was another side that needed to be brought to light.

"Look, Evan, there's a lot more to it than just that." Linwood told him.

Evan said, "What more could there be? She's responsible for the accident that killed my father and then acts like nothing happened.

Linwood replied, "That was the only way your mother could have ever lived with herself"

Linwood had never talked to anyone about this tragedy. He thought of it every day but chose not to talk about it. The memory was as fresh in his mind as if it just happened yesterday. He vividly remembered how that one phone call changed the way he would live the rest of his life.

Linwood continued, "Your mother was in deep depression. She couldn't bear to see me or my wife anymore. Part of your mama died that day too."

The look on Evan's face softened. He never had the slightest idea that she'd been wrestling with this throughout his entire life. Thinking he would hear good stories about his father that night, things had taken a sharp turn. He was learning something he had never known about his mother. He knew he had no clue how that must have been for her. He felt like he owed her an apology. For all this time, he thought his emotions were heavier and mattered more than anyone else's in his life.

Evan asked, "Why did she seem so surprised when I told her my uncle was gone too?"

"She probably was." said Linwood. He continued, "There was hope that he was going to survive. After brain trauma and nearly a year in a coma, he passed away."

Evan couldn't believe that he was the one to break the news to her. He had done it without even thinking anything of it. If he had only known all this time.

"I feel so guilty." Evan said, "I can't even imagine how that had to have been not just for her, but for you."

In response, Linwood said, "I have just not spoke about it much before. I have always tried to hide how it's impacted me until… until I was able to meet you."

Linwood knew how much this subject meant to Evan. He realized what knowing about his father meant to him. Evan had never even known what he even looked like until a few days ago. Knowing that, Linwood wanted to open up about not only his sons, but about himself.

"You remind me a lot of your father. You're determined, whether you know it or not. You wouldn't be here right now if you weren't. You knew you needed something, and you did whatever it took to find it."

To be characterized like his father meant a lot to Evan. It felt good to know he had gotten a positive trait from him.

Linwood asked, "So, do you have anyone special in your life?"

Evan replied, "Special? What do you mean?" Linwood answered, "A girl is what I mean."

Evan, surprised by this question, replied, "Oh, right. No, I don't. I've always been too busy for girls." He more honestly continued, "I guess I just haven't been able to connect with anyone else on an emotional level."

Evan didn't really care about that kind of relationship anymore. He felt like it would distract him from his goals. He had always been taught to put himself before others. He had become quite self-centered when it came to his personal friendships and relationships.

Evan's mind was racing so fast with thoughts that he just couldn't keep up with it. Evan had been in love before ... even engaged to his high school sweetheart, Angela Sanders. He had known her his whole life. They had a special connection. He was young and didn't have a worry in the world at that time. He had no reason for any. They had both gone to the same university. Everything had begun to make sense, and he thought his life was coming together. He thought he had everything he needed. Looking back, he realized that as he had become older and more in touch with the real world, things had started to change for him. Things didn't come easy anymore. Life challenges had begun to stare him in the face.

At twenty years old, he had thought he was ready to embark on a future of success. As the student body president of a university, he had taken on a great responsibility and had felt an enormous amount of pressure to live up to the mountain of expectations everyone had of him. Having a personal life was difficult during that time, so he had allowed himself to get the point that he didn't have one anymore. He had known that, if he didn't achieve a certain amount of success, his life would be viewed as a failure in the eyes of his family. He would have taken any chance he got to get away from that pressure. He had tried to make up for the lost personal time, but doing so had led him to a long road of regrets.

With all these thoughts rolling through his mind, Evan sat there with a blank look on his face. He looked as if he was both in a deep thought and just simply lost.

Linwood asked, "You okay?" Evan quickly shook his head as if to clear it of his current thoughts and back to reality.

He responded, "Yes! Yes! Do you have any regrets? You know, with your life ... your family?"

Linwood immediately straightened up in his chair and took a deep breath.

He said, "Well, thinking about it, I have found myself feeling guilty. It's not a good feeling to have."

"What do you mean?" Evan asked him.

Linwood replied, "I've had a lot of regrets when it comes to being a father. I spent so much time working, I wasn't there for them enough. In my mind there was always a tomorrow. I thought like that until, all of a sudden, everything changed … and there wasn't any more tomorrows for them. They were gone."

Evan was blown away by Linwood's honesty. He had never known anyone with the humility to admit their flaws. Evan saw the impact that loss had made on him. He felt it within himself, but had never seen it in another person. This new perspective made him realize the deep impact loss could have on someone's life. In this case, the opportunity Linwood had for time with his sons was gone … and so were they.

Evan thought about Angela. He had proposed to her at a very young age. Nobody but the two of them knew about it. He knew his family wouldn't approve due to his age and just the fact they didn't seem to put much value on love. They were engaged for over a year. Evan became more and more busy. There was never a right time to move forward with the relationship, but there came a moment when everything changed.

It all came back fresh to his mind. It was the annual Valentines Fraternity Social, and Evan had been swamped with school work and student government responsibilities. He was looking forward to a chance to get a little relief from his stress. His relationship with his fiancée, Angela, was beginning to become stale. It was only after he had a few drinks that their relationship would seem to come alive for him.

He remembered it well. Weeks later, he and Angela were alone in his apartment. What was on her mind was more important than anything else right then. It was just another normal day. Evan was studying for the LSAT and preparing to go to law school, but Angela had something on her mind. She knew she had to tell him. There wasn't any way for her to keep her secret much longer. She had no clue as to what his reaction would be, but what was on her mind was more important than anything else. Angela had tried on several occasions to discuss the future of their relationship and even mentioned the idea of getting married.

She finally worked up the courage to drag him away from his books. She didn't waste any time getting to the point this time. She let him know that she was ready to get married. From Evan's perspective, the conversation was pointless. The last thing he wanted to do was think about marriage at that time. She tried to reason with him, but he refused to listen. He got up to get back to what he thought of as "important things." She grabbed his hand and pulled him back toward her. With the other hand, she pulled a pregnancy test from her pocket.

Evan was confused. At first, he thought she was hinting that she wanted to start a family. He remembered her next words well: "Evan, we're having a child." Those words were tattooed in his memory. The word "we're" stood out explicitly. He didn't want anything to do with this. He was in disbelief. His spontaneous and thoughtless decisions had begun to catch up to him. A loud confrontation had followed and lasted a long time. The silent thoughts and feelings that had been growing in their relationship were completely unleashed. His selfish nature was revealed that day.

Angela had realized their toxic relationship brought too many struggles and was not worth fighting for. She had known the ring on her finger was not worth wearing any longer. Evan remembered how, with tears flowing down her face, she had looked at the ring he had given her nearly a year ago. Knowing it represented what used to be, she had walked over to the desk where he was sitting acting as if nothing had happened. He remembered being interrupted from his thoughts when Angela slammed her hand on the desk and scattered his papers. When she lifted her hand, he had seen the ring laying there. He remembered exactly the tone in her voice when she had said to him, "Whatever "was" is over. I've had enough."

Before he could say a word, she had made her way out the door. She had walked away from everything she had hoped for and the life she dreamed of having. Angela and his baby were gone. He remembered exactly the moment he decided that was the life he wanted ... a life where success would compensate for the things that truly mattered. Now thinking of it, he realized that his personal mistakes had left him alone ... and brought shame ... and sadness.

He and Linwood were still sitting there in front of the fire as it was beginning to die down.

Evan was lost in thought when Linwood spoke up, "Time goes by so quick. Any moment with someone you love should be valued. At this point in my life I just wish I had more of it, especially with my wife." With that, Linwood stood up as if he was trying to escape the emotional moment, "But, there's nothing that can be done about that. You know?" he continued.

Evan nodded his head in agreement. He knew that Linwood had no clue that what he had been saying had hit him deeply.

"How did you know?" Evan asked him.

"Know what?" said Linwood. "You know, that your wife was the one. How could you tell?"

Linwood sat back down and told him, "Well, I'll tell ya. One day someone will come into your life, and everything about them will be unforgettable. They'll never escape your mind ... you'll know."

Evan knew deep down that someone had already been in his life. His thoughts were captivated by her even after all these years. Everything she did, he remembered. Everything she said, he knew word for word. Time had not faded his feelings. All this time he had told himself to put the past behind him and to focus on the things that would bring himself glory. Over time that glory faded into shame, and it had filled his life to a point where it was hardly worth living.

The fire went completely out, and the only sign of light came from inside the cabin.

Linwood said, "Well, I think I'll go ahead turn in for the night."

Evan had lost track of what time it was. He had been so focused on their deep conversation and his many thoughts about the past. They both got up and made their way back inside the cabin where they would stay the night. Evan thought about taking his chair back with in him, but he knew he would be back out at the fire pit again. He knew that from now on there was a need for more than one chair in Linwood's life.

As they entered in the single room inside the cabin, the chilly air seemed to follow them. Linwood made his way to his small sleeping area against the wall.

He told Evan, "There is a mattress up there in the loft. Get all the blankets you need."

"Thank you." Evan replied, "Goodnight."

"Sleep well," Linwood responded back.

Evan went over to the other side of the room and grabbed a handful of blankets. He threw them up onto the mattress in the loft. It was completely dark in the room. He pulled out his phone flashlight and eased his way up the small ladder. He looked down and shined the light on Linwood who had already fallen asleep. It was as if he was in the best sleep of his life.

He noticed the time read *8:24 p.m.* on his phone. This was the earliest he remembered getting in bed in a long time. As he laid there, the mattress was surprisingly comfortable; but he was not. He couldn't help but think about how all the things had transpired in his life. He began to wonder what life would look like if he had thought of himself a little less. The mental images of himself as a groom and as a father loomed over him while he struggled to keep his eyes shut.

He knew that so many precious moments had been pushed out of his memory all these years. There were people with whom he could have shared them. There were people he could have loved and who would have loved him. He knew he needed to use this new-found determination that had brought him to this place …

to take him even farther… to find them.

Detour

Evan woke up and had to think about where he was. He nearly hit his head on the ceiling when he sat up in the loft of the cabin. The sound of the distant cars on the highway made an almost peaceful noise. The sky was still dark as the sun had yet to rise. It wasn't even seven o'clock. He had already gotten more than a full night's sleep.

He looked over to where he had last seen Linwood sleeping. He wasn't there. Evan carefully made his way down the ladder and walked out to the porch. He had fallen asleep wearing his jacket, and it still had the scent of smoke on it. The air was very cool as he looked out from the cabin's screened porch to where Linwood was sitting on the dock in his chair with his Bible in his hand and a cup of coffee on the table beside him. It was a peaceful sight

The "what if" thoughts that had kept him awake the night before crept back into Evan's mind. He didn't want to disturb Linwood, so he took a seat on the porch and watched the sunrise. His thoughts soon completely blocked his vision of the scene in front of him. The part of him that had said "forget and push aside" seemed to be gone. Now he was caught up in, not only what could have been, but what could be.

After several minutes passed, Linwood slowly made his way up from the dock. When he opened up the screen door and saw Evan sitting there.

He said, "Well, good morning to ya."

Evan replied, "Good morning." Linwood said, "We better be getting ready to go. I need to check and see if the farm is still there."

Evan knew he needed to resume his life as well. He had put everything on pause for the past several days. While he was able to find clarity about many things, there was now another area of his life that filled his mind with questions. He felt like he could never win the self-battle with which he fought. He had lived with uncertainty for so long and had hoped to eventually get to the bottom of it. He had learned a lot the last couple of days. In his mind, he now understood the person he wanted to be, and he knew it was up to him to become that person.

They got their things together, packed the truck, and made their way back to the farm. They drove what seemed like the never-ending dirt road and passed the same fields they had seen the day before. Evan sat quietly during the drive. He didn't know anywhere he would rather be. If it were up to him, he would have stayed in that moment for the rest of his life. He knew he didn't fit in that environment, but he knew he belonged with his grandfather. He belonged in a place away from everything he had ever known.

They got close to the farm, and he looked toward the highway again as they drove on the overpass. He knew he would be driving that road going back to Raleigh to assume the job for which he had worked so hard. He also knew it would be one of the hardest things he would ever have to do. He had a hard time seeing himself in that position. The attention just didn't matter anymore.

They made their way back onto Johnson Road and turned into the driveway where two pickup trucks were parked. Four guys came walking out of the barn. It was obvious that they had spent the morning working as their shirts and pants were already dirty. Linwood and Evan both got out of the truck, and Linwood began walking towards the men. James was one of them.

He saw Linwood and jokingly said, "Did you have a nice little break, Sir?"

"Indeed, very much so." Linwood replied.

James pointed to Evan, then turned to look at the other guys, and told them, "And this right here is the fella I was telling y'all about that drives that nice vehicle right there."

As the guys were looking at Evan's brand new car, he felt a little awkward and didn't know what to do other than to just stand there. The fact of being a misfit had arisen again ... a fact of which he had been completely made aware. As he pondered again his reason for being there, he couldn't fully understand how he could both love being at this place and, at the same time, feel so out-of-place.

"Well let's head on inside." Linwood told Evan.

The two of them entered through the side door of the farmhouse.

As he and Evan walked inside, Linwood asked Evan, "Can I get ya anything for breakfast?"

Evan, who by now didn't have much of an appetite, replied, "I'll just take a banana."

"That's it? You sure?" Linwood asked, as he handed him a banana.

Evan responded, "Yes, sir. I actually need to get going pretty soon."

"Well, don't rush off." Linwood insisted.

"I think I need to be making my way back up to Raleigh. I don't want to pay rent for an unused apartment" Evan said.

Linwood laughed, "I guess you have a point."

Evan scrambled through his bag that had the same rotation of clothes he had worn for the past several days. He found the picture that had led him to his grandfather and pulled it out. He had taped the two pieces together where he had torn it in half.

He handed Linwood the photo and said, "Here, I want you to keep this for me until I get back." "You don't have to do that." Linwood said.

Evan replied, "No, I think it'd be best if you keep it. It has gotten me far enough."

Linwood took a look at the picture and told Evan, "I'll take good care of it in the meantime."

As Evan headed toward the door, Linwood grabbed a piece of paper and a pen and jotted something on it.

Passing it to Evan, he said, "Here's my number, just in case you need it. Call me anytime."

Evan took the paper, tucked it in his pocket, and said, "Yes sir, of course."

Evan realized that he wasn't sure how to deal with the next moment. Having to say goodbye was one reason Evan had never wanted to get too close to anyone. Over this short period of time, he had never felt closer with anyone else in his life. The big job in the big city could never give him more than the reception he had received on this farm in the last few days. He had received a genuine welcome from Linwood. He had been happily received into in a place and into a life where he had never known he belonged.

Trying to avoid an emotional moment, Evan just wanted to turn his back and leave. He didn't want to say anything else. He opened the door and made his way outside toward his car. Linwood stood on the porch and watched him walk away. He felt like he'd watched too many people he loved leave. Then a heartfelt moment of reality began to set in for the both of them. The dream was over for now ... what they had both longed for was temporarily over.

Evan opened his car door and waved to Linwood. With a soft smile, Linwood waved back. Evan put his key in the ignition and started the car. Linwood watched as the car began to back out of the driveway. In that moment Evan's heart began to race, he couldn't leave like his grandfather like this. He knew he wouldn't be able to go any further at the moment. He owed more than a wave to the man who was changing his life. He braked the car and slipped it back in forward. Linwood was opening the door to the house. Evan put the gear in park and quickly got out of his car.

"Wait!" Evan said.

Linwood was caught by surprise. As he turned around, his first thought was that Evan must have left something. Evan did in fact leave something behind. It was something Linwood could have never seen coming.

Linwood asked him, "Leave something?"

Without saying anything, Evan walked up to his grandfather and immediately embraced him. Linwood, caught off guard, didn't have any idea what to say. All he knew to do was return Evan's hug.

"Thank you so much." Evan said to him. "You have forever changed my life in ways you can't even imagine."

Linwood couldn't quite understand what Evan meant by this. He had no idea that their conversation the night before had brought to light an important part of Evan's life that he had left behind. It was a part that was still missing in his incomplete puzzled state of mind.

Linwood said to him, "Love you, son."

He hadn't been able to say that to anyone in so long. Now he was not only able to say it but to also truly feel it … and to receive it.

Evan replied, "Love you too, Granddad."

Tears began to trickle from Linwood's eyes … he had never expected to hear those words. He wouldn't take anything for this moment. Evan had not heard those words in so long either, especially from someone truly meaning it. It meant more than anything to hear it from this man who meant so very much to him. Hearing it back from family … from the only piece of his father that he had, his grandfather.

Clearing his voice, Linwood said, "You better go if ya gonna beat that traffic."

Evan took a few steps back and wiped his face. He was lost in what had just taken place.

He said, "Yes sir, I guess I should."

Linwood held his hand out, and Evan shook it. Evan felt the strong grip of his grandfather's had just as he a few days before. They both turned and went their separate ways. As Evan walked back to his car, he felt content. He knew he wouldn't have been able to sleep if he had not had that moment. Evan started the engine once again and drove onto the country road. He had a long drive back to Raleigh … a lot of time to himself. He had all the time he needed for his mind to take him back to a place where he never thought he would go.

As Evan merged onto the busy highway, his peaceful feeling began to vanish. He started to wonder if he was making the right decision. He wondered if where he had in mind to go was really where he belonged. Somehow the senate seat he had worked so hard to gain just didn't seem all that important. The thoughts of Angela that he had rehearsed in his mind the night before filled his mind. His time with his grandfather at the cabin had created "what if" thoughts in his head. He tried to reason it out by telling himself that special moment was now over. As he continued to drive, it occurred to him that he wouldn't be returning back home for nearly another month.

He wondered if he could last that long with the questions that loomed over him now. The further he traveled, the more questions began to loom heavily over him. The part of himself that he had not wanted to remember captured his thoughts.

Evan knew where he belonged and where he wanted to be. Yet, he was going in the opposite direction of that places and those people. The family he had and the family he could've had were more distant the further he traveled. He thought about the uncertainty he had faced growing up. The uncertainty he had growing up was caused because he was without a father. He knew in his hear that his job and image were not worth causing another child to suffer the concerns that had always haunted him. Could he allow his own child to face such challenges?

Evan continued to drive, thinking of nothing else but what he was leaving behind. He was near the halfway point of the trip. He knew what he was thinking about doing would change things forever, but he just couldn't take it anymore. He would put everything at risk. Traveling at over 70 miles per hour, Evan saw an exit coming up on his right. He didn't want it to turn into another blur. Without slowing down at all, he immediately veered to the right, just barely making the exit. The sound of car horns beeping caught his attention, as he began to slow down. Evan couldn't believe what he had just done. He felt as if he had lost control and something else within him had taken over. Whatever that something was, he appreciated it. Evan knew there were so many things left incomplete. He couldn't do anything else without reaching out to them.

He turned left at the stoplight and made his way to the exit leading to the same route he had just left going in the opposite direction. His car engine revved up as he increased speed. Without thinking twice, he was headed back home. He was going completely against the norm that he had always followed. Evan was speeding back as if he was running away from something. He was! He was running away from all that he didn't want in life and toward the man he wanted to be. His eyes remained straight ahead focusing only on the road that was ahead of him. Redemption

was the only thing on his mind as he got closer to home. There wasn't an ounce of uncertainty in the decision he had made. He knew exactly where he was going and wasted no time in getting there.

As if he was on borrowed time, Evan quickly made his way through traffic and turned onto his neighborhood street. He sped up as he approached his grandparents' house. Almost hitting their mailbox, he pulled into the driveway as he had done so many times before. He immediately opened the car door and ran to the front steps of the house. As he reached in his pocket for the house key, the door opened. There stood his grandfather who said, "Evan? What are you doing here?" Evan didn't have a care in the world about what his grandfather had said. It didn't mean anything to him.

As he squeezed through the tight space between his grandfather and the door, Evan said to him, "Nice to see you too."

Before his grandfather could even turn around, Evan quickly made his way up the stairs and into his room.

His grandfather yelled to him, "Whatever you are doing, you're making a big mistake."

His grandfather's voice was silenced by the sound of his bedroom door slamming shut. Evan locked the door and walked over to his closet and turned on the light. It exposed the mess that was there. Suitcases, boxes, shirts and jackets on hangers ... the space was completely filled. Evan pushed some things out of the way and eased into the walk-in closet. He used a stool and reached up to the top shelf of the closet. He felt around, moving his hands from side to side on the shelf. Several hats came falling down before he finally felt the paper box.

He grabbed it and stepped down from the stool. He turned the box around and saw the words "*High School*" written on it. He opened it to find it was filled with old yearbooks, report cards, and pictures. He pulled out a prom picture of him and Angela. He looked at it, with the image bringing back so many memories from that time. He put the picture down and scrambled through the box one more time. He knew what he was looking for and it wasn't in there.

Evan moved the box aside and went into the closet again. He stood on the stool and reached up to the top shelf again. He saw another box that was there. This one was heavier. He carefully pulled from the shelf and saw the word "*College*" written on the outside. His eyes widened as he stepped off the stool. He put the box on the floor and knelt down beside it to open it. He hoped that what was inside would be the start of finding what he truly needed …

to help him regain what he had left behind.

The Search

The box had been there in his closet holding memories that Evan had avoided for so long. It hadn't been touched since he moved back from college. Not only was it now right in front of him, he knew the start of something amazing could be too. He slowly began to rip open the tape that sealed up the box. As it opened, it was noticeable that the items in the box were piled up to the top. Evan pushed them all aside and reached toward the bottom. He knew what he was looking for.

It was there just where he thought it would be … the yellow file folder. As he pulled it from the box, numerous letters and envelopes fell out of it. The letters had all been sent to him by the same person, Angela Sanders. Just seeing them all there before his eyes hit a very tender spot in his emotions. He remembered receiving them while being away at his summer internship during college.

Evan hadn't planned to read them. He just needed the address from which she had sent them. After Evan wrote the address on a small sheet of paper, he put it in his coat pocket. He started to put the letters back when he felt a strong urge to unfold one of the letters. He hadn't wanted to be taken into a world of memories, but he just couldn't help himself. He began reading and read through every note from start to finish. He had forgotten just about everything that was written in them. He caught himself smiling ear-to-ear as years of memories came flooding back. Feeling as if he was reliving every detail from their relationship, he also dealt with the shame of every detail of his past self. Back then he hadn't appreciated any of them. He remembered skimming through some of them and filing them away. He had eventually stopped even reading them at all … just tossing them in his desk drawer.

Angela had sent numerous letters to Evan over the summers and while he was in law school. The love letters she sent had turned more serious after she got pregnant. Evan remembered getting mail with her name on the envelope and not even bothering to open it. He was too ashamed. He knew how things had ended, and he knew it was all his fault. Avoiding the letters had been his way of trying to avoid the shame of the whole situation. He had thought it was all over, but now it was all right there in front of him. He had no choice but to face it.

Sitting there on his bedroom floor, he began to tear through the envelopes that were still sealed. When he opened the first one, a small picture was with the letter. Before reading, he looked at it. He saw it was an ultrasound picture with his child on it. The first part of the letter read, "It's a boy." Tears began to build up in his eyes and fell down his face. Seeing a glimpse of his son for the first time brought emotions he had never imagined.

The letters eventually stopped coming. Evan's lack of response to them had caused Angela to realize that Evan had no intention of being a part of their baby's life. She had, for a while, lived off the hope that he would come back not just in her life, but her sons. She decided to stop sending them after she sent a picture of their newborn son. Angela knew if he didn't respond then, he would never.

Reading the letters one by one, Evan realized that his plan had worked. He had succeeded in pushing Angela away. He had pushed away memories of all the amazing memories that had made and even the baby they had made. He had succeeded in missing out on so much happiness in his life. Evan now wondered whether his life would be different now if he had opened those letters when he got them. Maybe he wouldn't be on his bedroom floor alone and in tears now if he had. The tears he shed now were tears of shame and guilt instead tears of joy that he should have experienced at the birth of his son.

Evan wiped his tears with his shirt sleeve and pushed the letters aside. There was something else in the box he wanted. He opened the box up again and reached down to the very bottom. "It has to be in here…" He thought to himself as he scrambled around through the box again. Without looking, he moved his hand to the bottom corner inside the box. Then he felt it. A small square box.

Evan pulled it out, held it up close to his eyes, and read the outside of the box. It was labeled "*Tiffany & Co.*" He slowly opened the box, and what was inside of it glittered in the dimly lit room. This was the ring that he had rebelliously bought at such a young age … the ring that Angela had once worn on her finger. Evan thought back to the day when he had last seen it. He remembered sitting at his desk and holding it after Angela had left. Her returning the ring had been the final goodbye to everything he and Angela had been to each other. He knew what he had done. It has been his choice. Filled with frustration and despair, he had closed the ring box and thrown it into the box that was in his apartment. It was this same box that had stored years of memories and hadn't seen the light of day for a long time.

Evan had relived all the memories and regained the feelings that he had erased from his mind. His blurred vision of life when he was younger had been cleared. He could see past his own needs now … and into those of Angela and their son. There was so much that needed to be said. He had kept quiet for far too long. Finding Angela would be the beginning to making right the wrongs he had done.

Evan got himself together and put all of the letters back into the box and closed it. He got up from the floor, picked the box up and took it back into the closet. He put it back into place like it hadn't been touched. There was one thing that didn't make it back into the box. The small ring box was still sitting there on the floor. Evan had unintentionally forgotten to store it back inside the big box. He bent down to pick it up and took a long look at it.

As he stood there holding the ring box in his hand, the sound of a knock came from the outside of his door.

"You in here Evan?" It was his mother asking.

He quickly covered the ring box in his hand and placed it in his coat pocket. His mother had no clue that he was ever engaged to Angela. She had never known the real reason why they split up. Evan had kept those personal matters from everyone.

He walked over to the door and opened it. "Yes?" he said.

She replied, "What are you doing here? I thought you'd be in Raleigh."

Evan shrugged his shoulders, "Yeah. I thought so, too."

He stood there thinking how drastically everything can change so quickly. He knew that no prior schedule or plan could get in the way of where he was meant to be. He also knew that there was no way he could tell his mother what Linwood had told him the night before. Evan did his best to not let on to his mother what was going on in his mind. He was trying to appear the same as he usually did with her; but, in reality, everything was completely different. His feelings of sympathy and a new understanding for his mother had grown to new heights. He tried very hard to look in her eyes in the way he had always done. It was nearly impossible.

"Things change," said Evan.

His mother replied, "Evan…Honey, you just don't understand."

He told her, "I understand more now than I ever have about so many things, especially myself."

She wasn't able to grasp what he meant. There were so many things that she didn't know about her son. When they looked each other in the eyes, they both had different perceptions. She saw someone that she didn't really know anymore. He saw somebody that he knew better than ever before. She felt as if they had become strangers when in fact her son had truly never felt closer to her.

His mother said to him, "Well, do what you think is best."

Evan replied, "I know it is best. I promise."

That was all he could say in that moment. Evan knew the time would come where light would be shed on all the things that were left unsaid. He believed that there was so much more out there that he could show her. It was his job to find it. For so long he thought he had reached a dead end in his life. It wasn't until his eyes had been opened to the unknown things that he could think differently. It was like a long road with no ending. There was more ahead of him, the greater and everlasting things of life.

He bent down and kissed his mother's cheek and walked on past her. She stood still as Evan made his way towards the staircase. She didn't have any idea where he was going. What she did know was that wherever it was, he cared about it. To her, that was all that mattered now.

As Evan walked down the stairs, he put one hand on the stair rail and the other in his left coat pocket. He felt the ring box and the small piece of paper. Those were the only two things he needed to find the person he needed the most. He moved with purpose, not wanting to lose any more time away from where he felt like he was supposed to be. Reaching the bottom of the staircase, he reached his hand out for the door. Before he could even touch the handle, a hand pressed against the door. He recognized his grandfather's watch on his wrist, and he slowly turned around to see him standing there.

"I can't let you do this. You'll make a fool out of this family…Out of me. I can't even begin to…"

"Let him go!" Evan's mother interrupted, with a determined tone in her voice.

Evan looked up to see her standing at the top of the stairs. She was nervously breathing heavy. His mother rarely spoke up for anything or anybody, especially to her father. What caused her to do this was the love she had for her son. The two of them weren't the best at showing it, but it was there. She couldn't bear to see him unhappy any longer. She knew what unhappiness was like. She lived with it every day.

His grandfather's face showed utter disbelief. He had always been in control of everything in his family's lives. In that moment, he realized he had completely lost it. With his hand still on the door, Evan gently and slowly moved it off. He looked into his grandfather's eyes and saw a stare that reached into his soul. Without saying a word, Evan opened the door and left.

Evan felt a sense of new-found freedom as he walked away from a burden that had always been cast upon him. He opened his car door, slid in and sat in silence. He needed a moment to bring his mind back to reality … a moment to calm his spirit as he was about to begin a mission that to most would seem impossible.

Evan took a good look at the small sheet of paper with the address written on it. He thought to himself, "This is it!" He still felt a sense of uncertainty. What if she had moved? What if she was married? Those "what ifs" seemed pretty reasonable after years of no communication with someone. Yet, they didn't change Evans's mind. Instead, he determined to imagine positive scenarios. He pictured all the things that he could hope for. After he entered the address on his phone and began to make his way, he realized that he didn't really need directions. It was like he knew exactly where to go. After taking one turn, he could remember making the same drive so many times years ago. It all became more and more familiar as he got closer. It was like a light was shining down on the road in front of him telling him where to go. He was well on his way.

Cypress Road was written on the paper; and before he knew it, that was his next turn. Before turning onto the road, his nerves began to act up. He was becoming anxious. He didn't know what he would say to her or whoever would open the door. Evan started to realize that one complete stranger could immediately crush his hopes within a split second. All he could hope for was the best.

He drove slowly down the street. There were houses on both left and right. Evan didn't need to look for the numbers on the mailboxes. He knew exactly where it was. He continued on almost reaching the end of the street, and there it was to his left. The house that he had seen so many times was right there in front of him. The nervousness that Evan felt reached a new height. The moment had arrived. There was no turning back.

Evan put his car in park and closed his eyes. He took a deep breath and opened the car door. He got the same feeling he had when walking towards his Aunt Cynthia's house. He made his way onto the front sidewalk. He was going over what he'd say in his head. Evan slowly went up the front steps, and with his knees were buckling, he made it onto the front porch. The thoughts and the nerves all came to a pitch as he reached out and touched the doorbell. With both of his hands behind his back, he rocked back and forth.

After what felt like an eternity, the door opened. Evan hadn't seen the tall, thick armed man who appeared before him in years. The man who he once feared. That fear slowly started to creep back. It was the same man who gave him the hardest handshake he ever had in his younger years. Evan once knew him as "Mr. Sanders" … Angela's father. He didn't quite recognize Evan at first. "Do I know you?" He asked Evan.

"Um.. Well, it has been awhile." Evan replied.

Mr. Sanders asked, "Last name?"

Evan said, "Stevenson. Evan Ste-"

Evan couldn't finish. He saw the look on Mr. Sanders' face, and it said it all. It was obvious that he knew who he was, and most importantly.. what he did. It was a look of disappointment mixed with anger.

"And just what do you think you're doing here?" Mr. Sanders asked.

Evan took a few steps back and said, "Sir, I've made a lot of mistakes. I- I just want to know how Angela's doing."

Mr. Sanders wasn't buying it. He said, "Angela is doing just fine nowadays. I think it'd be best for her to stay that way."

Evan didn't say anything. He wondered if everything was starting to fall apart. He felt lower than he ever had in his life. Just then a voice came from inside of the house.

"Hun, who is it? Your food is in here getting cold."

Mr. Sanders turned his head and said back, "One second. I'll be right there."

He looked at Evan, who's eyes were beginning to water. All he could do was stand there helpless.

Mr. Sanders said to Evan, "Look, I don't know how to help you. That's the nicest way to say it." With that, he closed the door soundly.

Evan begged, "No…no. Sir please, you can't"

The door was shut, and that was it. This was the dead end to what seemed like a never-ending road of a new life for Evan. It was over. With his emotions beginning to take over, he lost it. He completely broke down. Evan slowly turned around facing the front yard and took a seat on the front steps. He put this hands over his face and wept.

As Mr. Sanders looked through the door window and saw Evan torn apart, he couldn't help but feel a little sorry for him. He made his way over to the kitchen table where his wife was there waiting for him.

"Who was that?" she asked him.

"The Stevenson boy." he replied.

Her eyes widened, "As in…"

"Yes, Evan." he told her.

Hearing this, she was completely caught off guard.

She said to him "Did you really have to slam the door on him?"

"What else was there to do? Can you think of any other solution?" he asked her.

"Well, did he say anything?" she asked.

Mr. Sanders thought for a minute, and he replied, "There's nothing worthwhile that boy can say."

Mrs. Sanders did not know how to react at first, but something gave her a feeling that she never thought she'd feel. She was concerned that her grandson did not have a father in his life. In that moment, she could imagine a smile on her grandson's face that only Evan, his father, could give him. She knew this was no time for backs to be turned. As she got up from the table, her husband gave her a questionable look. She didn't say anything as she walked over to the door.

Several minutes had gone by, but Evan was still sitting on the steps crying. In the midst of sniffling and tears, he heard the door open. Embarrassed and hurting, he knew he couldn't turn face Mr. Sanders again so he kept his head on his knees. He heard footsteps on the front porch coming behind him. Evan just knew that he'd hear Mr. Sanders telling him to leave. The footsteps got closer, and he felt the presence of someone sitting beside him.

Without lifting his head, he heard a voice. "Look, Evan. The door shouldn't have been shut on you. You weren't able explain yourself." Mrs. Sanders said to him.

Evan lifted his head but couldn't say anything. He nodded his head and tried to avoid Ms. Sanders' eyes. Ms. Sanders put her hand on Evan's shoulder. Seeing the tears flow down Evans red face explained everything she needed to know.

Seeing a different Evan from the one she remembered, Mrs. Sanders said to him, "You deserve to be heard. I can't promise anything, but this is all we can really tell you."

He couldn't avoid Ms. Sanders' eyes any longer. He turned to see her holding a small sheet of paper. Written on it were the words, "*Cedar Hills.*" Evan wasn't quite sure what this meant, but he was appreciative of any hint that would get him to Angela.

She told Evan, "She needs you. They need you. There's only so much her dad and I could do. It's up to you now."

Evan didn't know what to say or what to think. Ms. Sanders stood up from the step and reached her hand out to Evan. She helped him up and embraced Evan. Ms. Sanders realized that time could heal many things and many people as it did for Evan. What she also knew was that time couldn't mend the emptiness her daughter and her grandson felt… only Evan could do that.

She said to Evan, "Now go."

… *and Evan went.*

Encounter

Evan had experienced a lot of unimaginable things in the past several days. However, nothing could have ever prepared him for what just happened. He hadn't seen this moment coming. He walked down the front steps of the house where Angela grew up, and he turned around to take another look. He saw Mrs. Sanders going back in the front door where her husband was standing waiting for her. Mr. Sanders had a questioning look on his face as his wife walked past him. He gave Evan a deep stare as he was closing the door. Evan realized that his mistakes had not only affected his life but others as well. He had not only hurt Angela, but also her family. They had been put into the position of being grandparents and also filling in the role he should have taken. He now wanted to make things right ... not only for the good of himself, but for everyone he had disappointed.

Evan didn't really understand what a major toll helping take care of a young child had taken on their relationship with their daughter. The name of the neighborhood where she lived was all the information they had about her to tell Evan. It was all they knew. Ever since Angela moved out, her parents hadn't heard from her. She was in her mid-twenties now wanting to be on her own and ready to escape her old lifestyle. A promotion at work had allowed her to do that.

Evan drove out of the neighborhood and went toward what he considered the unknown. As he drove farther and farther, he began to second guess the address on the sheet of paper that Mrs. Sanders had given him. He had no clue where he was. He wondered if he had been just using that to get rid of him. He really didn't understand why she would have been nice to him or why her opinion about him would have changed so quickly. He wondered if it really had changed or whether this address would lead him on a wild goose chase. Like he often had to do, Evan had to clear his mind and get his thoughts focused again on finding Angela.

Before he knew it, the voice on his phone sounded, "Your destination is on the right." He turned into the neighborhood and passed a sign that read *Cedar Hills*. He had no clue where to go from there. It seemed like there were hundreds of houses in the subdivision. He wondered if Angela's mother couldn't have told him anymore about where she was … or if she didn't want him to know more. Maybe she thought he'd give up. He didn't have a clue about the real reason.

The weather was nice, and lots of people were outside enjoying the unseasonably warm day. The friendly sight of children on the sidewalks riding their bikes and running eased his mind as he drove past them. He was trying to leave his extreme doubts and assumptions behind him.

Evan neared the cul de sac at the end of the street. He stopped his car and sat back in his seat to observe the neighborhood. He didn't know what to do next. He decided some fresh air might help, so he got out of the car and began walking down the sidewalk. A lone young boy was kicking a soccer ball not far from where a group of other kids were laughing and playing together. As Evan walked past the yard where the boy was playing with the soccer ball. it ricocheted off the goal and rolled into the street. The young boy stood still as he watched the ball roll away. Evan already felt bad for him because he was alone, so he figured the least he could do was get the ball for him. Evan called out to him, "I'll get it, buddy"

Evan looked both ways before running out onto the street where he retrieved the boy's ball. He walked back toward the yard with the ball in his hands.

The boy said to him, "You aren't supposed to touch it!"

For a second, Evan was confused … until he remembered the game rules. He tossed the ball down on the pavement and kicked it back to the boy's yard.

"You missed!" yelled the boy.

Evan realized this young kid just wanted someone to play with him. He thought to himself, "I've got a few minutes … why not?"

As he walked closer to the boy, he found his steps slowing to a complete standstill. He took a few steps back and looked at the boy. He recalled the look that Linwood Johnson had given him and felt as if he were seeing this boy the same way. The young boy looked familiar. His thick black hair and blue eyes stood out more than anything else. He looked like someone he had seen before. His observation was cut short when the young boy yelled, "C'mon!"

Evan didn't have much experience with kids and really didn't know much to say to the him. All he knew to do was kick the soccer ball back to him. Still, he just couldn't help but keep looking at him. Evan felt like he was familiar with those eyes, like he had seen them so many times before. He kept trying to brush the thought from his mind. He knew what he was thinking just couldn't be true.

The boy broke the silence by asking, "What's your name?"

For the first time ever, Evan had to think of his name. "Uh…Evan, it's Evan. What's yours?" he asked the boy.

The boy answered, "My name's Mason."

That name stuck in Evan's mind as Mason ran around the yard with a big smile on his face. It was as if the moment they had just shared had brightened Mason's personality. Evan was sure that whoever was in charge of this kid would freak out if they saw a complete stranger in their yard with him.

He curiously asked, "So, who is your legal guardian?"

Mason laughed and asked, "Huh?"

Evan had forgotten that he was talking to a child, so he rephrased the question, "Where are your parents?"

"My mom's inside getting ready for another date."

"Oh really?" Evan wondered.

His mind raced once again as he realized that Mason hadn't mentioned anything about a dad. Suddenly the sound of a door opening and shutting from inside the garage interrupted their play. Evan's attention then focused in that direction. He heard the sound of what sounded like the click of high heels shoes getting closer. He turned his head back around so as not to stare at whomever was approaching. He kicked the ball back toward Mason whose laughter muffled the sound of the footsteps.

"Mason! Mason!" a voice yelled from the garage.

"Out here, Mom!" Mason yelled back.

"What did I tell you about going outside by yourself?" his mom asked him.

Mason replied, "I'm not, Mom!"

Evan was still facing the opposite direction from where she had walked out of the garage.

Mason enthusiastically ran toward his mother and said, "Mom! I made a friend!"

She was surprised, as she turned the corner, to see a man in her yard. "Hello? Who are you?" she concernedly asked Evan.

Evan stood still and closed his eyes. He had heard that voice so many times before. She had stopped and was standing still in her tracks. Recognizing the familiar back of Evan's thick black hair, her voice began to tremble as she asked again, "Who are you?" Evan slowly turned around. There she was ... just as beautiful as he had remembered her. The tall blonde-haired beautiful Angela Sanders was standing there right in front of him. His heart was about to pound through his chest. All of the reminiscing he had done had led him to this moment, but he hadn't expected it to happen like this.

Angela's face said it all ... a look of complete shock! However, with her son standing there, she knew she could not fully express the emotions she felt. There were so many thoughts running through her mind that she didn't know what to feel. She had so many questions, but that was not the time to ask them.

All she could say was, "Well... What a surprise!"

Evan was also at a loss for words. He, too, had so much to say but it couldn't be said with their son standing there with them.

There were a few seconds of awkward silence between them as they stood facing each other.

Evan finally spoke up, "So, date night?"

Angela answered, "Yes, actually it is. I have been calling around to find a sitter for Mason. They're so hard to find around here."

Mason spoke up immediately, "Please mom, can Mr. Evan do it tonight?"

To hear his own son call him "Mr" pained Evan. It was one thing for his employees to call him "Mr" … but his own son? That hit him hard. He hoped it didn't show on his face.

"Oh. I don't know about that." Angela answered.

Both Evan and Angela were trying to play it cool. They both knew they had a lot to discuss in private, but for the moment this had to seem like a normal encounter.

Needing to leave soon, Angela said, "Well maybe you could? My date will be here any minute now."

Evan inwardly felt hesitant as everything was happening so quickly.

Knowing that he couldn't just leave, he took a deep breath and said, "Okay. Okay, I will."

Hearing this made Mason's day. Evan had already won Mason over by simply playing with him. After all, he was just a young boy who didn't make friends easily. He wasn't good with communicating with kids his own age. He wasn't the kid everyone sat with in the lunchroom. Especially now, living in a fairly new neighborhood, he often found himself alone. Seeing Mason's excitement made Evan feel more at ease.

Soon a car pulled in the driveway. "Well, it looks like he's here" said Angela.

The man got out of the car and walked over the lawn to join them. Looking from Angela to Evan, he seemed a little skeptical at seeing a young, good looking man in Angela's front yard with them.

He mustered up a smile and asked her, "So who is this guy?" Trying to keep her composure, Angela replied. "This is Evan. He is Mason's sitter for tonight."

Evan couldn't help but think to himself, *"Here I am … a lawyer and state senator being introduced as a sitter."* As that thought ran through his mind, another one quickly followed. This new job title as "Mason's sitter" far outweighed any other that he had right then.

Angela took him from his thoughts as she said, "Mason will show you around the house, I'll be back before too late. Be ready to explain yourself."

Evan nodded and replied, "Okay, I understand. You just worry about having a nice time tonight" as he and Mason headed inside while Angela and her date walked toward the car.

Evan glanced out the window as Angela and her date drove off. He remembered all the times he had picked her up at her parents' home. The memories made seeing her with another man hurt his heart. He wished he had done things differently years ago. Things would have been so much different if he had. His life would have been so much better.

As the car went out of sight, he turned around to get a view of the living room. He walked around looking at the few pictures she had hanging. Most of them were of Angela and Mason. "Mr. Evan, come in here!" Mason called.

"Okay, but for now, please just call me Evan."

He said "for now" with hopes of him soon being able to call him "Dad." He felt in his heart that day would come. Learning about his son was one thing. Learning how to be a father was something that he knew would take time.

Mason led Evan down the hallway and into his bedroom. He flipped on the light and immediately the dinosaur/soccer themed room came alive. He immediately ran over to his basket of dinosaur action figures and proudly showed each and every one off to Evan, naming them one by one. Evan was just taking it all in.

He noticed a soccer poster on Mason's wall, and asked, "You really like soccer too, don't you?"

Mason replied, "Yeah, but there's really nobody to play with."

"I saw a lot of kids playing in the neighborhood today. What about them?" Evan asked.

"I think I'm invisible to most of them." Mason said softly.

Evan felt heartbroken to hear Mason say that. He knew that he would do anything he could to make up for the time he had missed with Mason and to make him believe that he belonged.

He quickly changed the subject and said, "Are you hungry."

Mason replied, "Mac & Cheese would be nice."

Evan sat there for a moment thinking that it indeed would be, and then it hit him, "Oh, I guess I need to make that." Mason followed him to the kitchen and saw the Mac and Cheese package his mother had placed on the counter. A note was taped to it for the sitter: *Dinner: This is about all he likes to eat these days.* Fortunately, it was the kind that only had to be heated in the microwave, so it didn't take long. Once it was ready, Mason sat down to eat his food. Evan went into the living room, sat in the recliner, and turned on the television. He hadn't just simply sat down and relaxed like that in so long. He flipped the channel to his favorite station for the news.

Within a few minutes Mason joined him with the remains of his bowl of Mac & Cheese in hand. He sat down on the end of the couch which was near where Evan sat in the chair.

He was quiet for a few minutes before asking, "Can we change the channel?"

Evan looked toward the bowl in his hand and said, "Are you even allowed to eat in here?"

Mason, grinning, replied, "I don't make a mess."

Evan, chuckling at his response, picked up the remote, Pressing the channel guide button, he asked Mason, "So, what do you want to watch?"

"I've got it." Mason said as he reached for the remote in Evan's hand.

He took it, stood up, and flipped through the channels the way he had done many times before. Evan just sat looking him over. He couldn't help but grin. Mason had a bowl of Mac & Cheese in one hand and the remote in the other. Evan realized in that moment that Mason's wishes would come first and he would be completely fine with it being that way.

With Nickelodeon now on, Evan picked up the empty bowl from the table and took it into the kitchen. After rinsing it out, he went back into the living room and sat back down on the couch beside Evan. He never could've imagined himself doing this, but now he knew he really wouldn't want to be anywhere else. He could tell that Mason appreciated his time and the fact that he had someone to sit there with him. It really didn't matter to him that the only thing he knew about him was his name. What mattered to him was that someone cared enough to spend time with him. That didn't happen very often.

As the time went by and while Mason's channel still played, Evan caught himself nodding. He couldn't let himself fall asleep … after all, he was the sitter. He looked over at Mason who was now lying down fast asleep beside him on the couch. He sat there briefly just taking in the sight of his son inhaling and exhaling. It was a sight that warmed his heart. After a few moments, he got up and gently lifted Mason from the couch into his arms. Not wanting to awaken him, he tiptoed down the hallway and into his bedroom. After he had laid him down on his bed and pulled the covers over him, Evan stood back and looked at his son. He felt the lump grow in his throat and the tears form in his eyes as he thought to himself, "Wow, that's my son! Right here in front of me is my son."

That was the first "dad" moment Evan had. He had not been there to hold him as a new-born baby nor to watch him take his first steps, but he knew for certain now that he never wanted to miss another big moment in Mason's life. He tiptoed across the room, pulled Mason's door closed, and went back into the living room. Just as he sat down and was changing the TV channel back to the news, he heard a car pull into the driveway. In a moment he heard Angela's footsteps. Evan stood up to greet her, trying to play it as cool as he possibly could. As she was unlocking the door, he felt frozen in place like an anxious father waiting for his child to come home at night. When the door opened, Evan couldn't help but notice the expression on Angela's face. There had been a time in their past when he didn't care how she felt, but right then he was genuinely concerned.

"You okay?" he asked her.

Angela took a few seconds to reply and finally said, "Oh. Yeah, I am. This is just a strange situation."

Since Angela had been on her own, she had tried to develop a more social lifestyle. For so long, her life had been focused on Mason. The majority of the time she had him alone, and it had taken a lot out of her. She had recently been making time to spend with different people, and she usually enjoyed her time out. However, something was different on this night out. She had been in a state of shock from seeing Evan and that was the only thing she could think of that whole evening with her date. She still felt like she was in a daze.

Evan asked again, "Angela. Are you okay?"

She put her hands over her face and, speaking in a loud voice, said, "I just don't know. This is all just too much. Why are you here? How did you even find us?"

"Shhh!" Evan said, cutting off her words as he moved closer to her.

He didn't want Mason awakened by this conversation. By this time, Angela's emotions had risen to the of tears that had welled up in her eyes. Evan walked even nearer to her and hesitantly wiped the tear that began to flow down her cheek with his thumb.

He pushed her hair back over her shoulder, and looking straight into her eyes and asked, "Are you okay now?"

Angela felt very vulnerable in that moment, but the past still stood between them. She still had so many questions, but she didn't really know if she was quite ready for the answers yet. The only thing she wanted to know for sure was that someone would be there …

and Evan was.

A Room Away

Evan and Angela both found themselves in an awkward moment as they stood face to face with Evan's hand on her shoulder. Angela didn't know how she should react. She felt herself easing closer to him; but, before he could embrace her, she quickly backed away. It seemed that she was battling between what she wanted to do and determining the right thing to do.

When she gained her composure, she said, "I really need to get to bed."

As she turned to walk away, Evan couldn't come to terms with what had just happened. Everything that had happened that night with Mason and the last few minutes with Angela had been like a good dream and now he was having to awaken from it.

"Oh. Yeah, I guess it is getting late." he said.

Reality set in as, standing there, he realized he had no place to go to spend the night. All he knew to do, though, was walk out the door into the night and leave, and so that is what he did. Everything was dark except for the street lights that shined dimly leaving his shadow behind him. He slowly walked toward his car that was still parked on the side on the road. Evan didn't know what was next. He knew he had been so close to what he had been looking for. Now, he had no choice but to walk away. The only place he knew to go was home. Evan couldn't believe he had come all this way just to turn back around and go home. He felt like he belonged here ... in a place where he truly wanted to be. However, all he knew to do now was go back to the place where he felt like misfit. It was a place he so desperately wanted to avoid.

Evan reached his car door and put his hand in his pants pocket for his car keys. He moved his hand around to find that they weren't there. After trying the other pocket, he slammed his hand on the roof of his car in frustration. He leaned over against the car and laid his head down on his arm. He needed a few minutes to get himself together. He was embarrassed, tired and cold … and standing on the street knowing he must have left his car keys in Angela's house.

With barely enough energy to make it back, he slowly climbed back up the steps to Angela's porch and approached the front door. He lifted his hand to knock on the door, but Angela opened the door before he could do so. Angela, still in her red dress, stood there holding his keys in her hand. She had watched him leave the house through her window. It had been easy for her to see his obvious frustration and disappointment.

"I see you forgot something." she said.

Without saying anything, Evan just nodded his head.

"Well, it took you long enough to come back for them." she said as she handed him the keys.

"I'm sorry." Evan said, "You can go on to bed."

Evan was noticeably tired as he stood there in front of her. He turned around and started to walk down the porch steps.

"Where are you planning to go?" she asked him. Evan held his hands up and said, "Home, I guess."

As Angela watched him walk to his car again, she knew she couldn't let him leave. She couldn't believe what she was. about to do. She didn't know why she was going to do it, but it felt right. It was what she needed to do.

"Wait a minute" she called out to him.

As Evan stopped walking and looked back at her, Angela said, "Just stay here tonight."

Evan turned around and replied, "I really shouldn't."

Angela gave him that familiar look that he had seen so many times before. It was a look that could not be denied.

"Well, if you're offering, I guess I will." Evan responded.

She opened the door wider and waved her hand for Evan to come in. He made his way back up the front steps and gave her a bit of a smile as he entered in the house. He immediately walked over to the couch where he stretched out. All he wanted to do was sleep.

Angela disappeared and came back saying, "Here's a blanket and pillow for you."

As she reached out to him with the blanket, she realized that Evan had already dozed off. She gently placed the blanket over him and stood back to look at him as he looked so peaceful lying there.

Angela could not believe that Evan Stevenson was there ... in her home, asleep on her couch. She never thought she would see nor hear from him again, but there he was. She felt the least she could do was to let him stay. He had put a smile on the face of her son like she had never seen before. His expression, as he had played with Evan, had shown her a spark of hope for Mason's happiness.

Angela walked down the hallway and into her bedroom. She was completely overwhelmed and had no idea what to do next. So many thoughts rushed through her mind as she pulled back the covers and got into her bed. She thought about how many nights she had gone to bed with no one lying beside her. She had been on her own and had convinced herself that she didn't really need anybody. She had thought she had everything she needed ... until something she didn't have was there in front of her. She wondered what would happen when she woke up. Would it be back to her normal schedule and normal life? Was that enough? Was that the life she wanted? These were the same questions that had been going through Evan's mind for weeks.

The next morning Angela was awoken by a noise coming from the kitchen. She looked at the clock on the nightstand ... it read *5:56 a.m.* It was only four minutes before her alarm would go off. She pushed the button down and got up to get ready for work. The mornings were usually hectic for her as she had to get both herself ready for work and her son ready for his day. It was not easy, but she had adapted to it. She had known that living on her own with a child wouldn't be easy when she left her parents' home, but she didn't want to have to be dependent on them anymore. She wanted to prove to herself and them that she didn't need any help.

After getting her bath and dressing, she opened her bedroom door to the sounds and smell of something cooking coming from the kitchen. She quietly walked down the hallway and peeked her head into the kitchen. There was Evan scrambling eggs with a plate of bacon and pancakes on the counter.

"What's all this?" Angela asked.

Evan turned toward her to say, "Oh this? Just a thank you for giving me a place to stay."

With a confused look on her face, she said, "Oh, right"

She stood there for a moment trying to take in what has happening. This wasn't a regular Monday morning. This wasn't her life.

She went back down the hallway and slowly opened the door to Masons room to wake him. As she did every morning, she gave him a soft tap on his shoulder.

"Time to get up." she said to him.

Mason's eyes slowly opened, and he immediately asked, "Mom, did you cook?" She replied, "No, but Evan .."

"Evan?!" He said, cutting her words off and sitting up in his bed.

Showing more energy than he ever had at that time of the day, he ran past his mother, out of his room, and into the kitchen. His eyes lit up when he saw Evan there dumping eggs onto a plate. This breakfast was much different than his usual Pop Tart in the toaster.

"Good morning, Buddy!" Said Evan.

Mason still wasn't sure who this guy was. All he knew was that he had played with him and now had cooked breakfast. He wasn't complaining. As Evan handed him a plate, Mason took it to the kitchen table and began to eat. Evan turned around to see Angela walking it the kitchen. "What can I fix for you?" He asked to which she replied, "Can we talk for a minute?"

Evan put down the plate and followed her into the hallway, away from where their son was eating.

"What's up?" He asked.

"What do you think you're doing?" Angela whispered to him.

"What do you mean?" He responded.

He was confused and thinking this couldn't be the same person that he saw last night.

"You think you can come here out of nowhere and then try to step in and take my place? Before Evan could respond, Angela continued, "Don't think I don't remember what happened."

Evan responded, "Look, I'll be out of your way in a few minutes. I just wanted to do something to thank you."

Evan began to walk back in the kitchen and then turned around to her and said, "Mason needs somebody…he really does."

"Does he? Or do you?" she asked.

He nodded his head and replied, "We both do."

As he started to turn around again, Angela thought about her son and how different he had acted the day before and that morning. A good different! Angela thought of the look on his face when she had said Evan's name and the image of the two of them in the front yard came to her mind. She knew it would be selfish of her to keep that from her son … and to keep that from the father of her son.

"Wait" she told him. He stopped and slowly turned back toward her. "You're right." She said, "He needs somebody, and I think it's you; but I'm telling you, that's it! Don't think anything more than that."

Evan responded by nodding his head. Nothing else needed to be said. He walked back into the kitchen and saw Mason sitting there eating his breakfast. Evan just couldn't help but smile, thinking of all the possibilities and moments that were now possible.

The coming weeks were just as Angela had said they would be. Evan drove the distance to her home almost on a daily basis. As soon as Mason got off the bus, instead of the usually nanny, it was Evan who was there waiting. Spending the afternoons together included playing soccer … but only after Mason's homework was finished. Homework was something Mason had always struggled with doing. Angela was accustomed to getting home to it not being done and it taking them into the night to finish. It was different when Evan told him to do it. There a was a different kind of respect that Mason had for him. He saw Evan in a way he wasn't able to view anybody else.

Angela had begun to come home every day to the sound of laughter and smiles in the front yard. Seeing that filled her heart with joy, but she was careful to put a serious look on her face as she got out the car and try not to show any sign of emotion. What had earlier been an honest emotionless look slowly became a facade. She didn't want it to be evident to Evan that change had begun to arouse in her heart. A change that was all because of him.

Every day when she got out of her car and walked to the house, she captured Evan's attention. Every time he looked at her and wished for that smile he had once known … the smile that he had once taken away from her. He didn't know that Angela couldn't help but look out the window to watch him and Mason playing together. He didn't know that every time she did it, that smile never failed to come alive. She only allowed it when she was alone so nobody could see it. The sad and lonely young boy she used to know had disappeared, along with the worries she had for him. They all went away, but the only change that Angela was willing to accept was the change Evan had made in her son.

Evan and Angela didn't really have much interaction, as most of his time at her house was spent with Mason. Evan respected Angela's wish for their relationship to be only about Mason. There were times when they caught each other's eye, but neither could admit it was anything more than happenstance. This went on for some time until one day when they couldn't avoid each other any longer. Evan had arrived at Angela's house early that afternoon as he usually did. He noticed her car in the driveway. He knew something was strange as she was never home this early. Evan got out of his car and rang the doorbell. He stood there for a moment waiting, but no one came to the door. He rang it again. Shortly after pressing the doorbell the second time, the door opened. Angela stood there still wearing her pajamas.

"Oh, sorry to disturb." Evan said.

"No, you're fine. Come on in" she said to him. Evan walked in and said, "Guess I'm a little early." "A little." She responded

It was like Evan had a little too much time on his hands. He always got there early because he had nowhere else to go and nothing else to do. For his whole life, he had kept busy and there was something on the agenda every day. Now his entire day revolved around being with his son. It was not only about just being with him but also about learning how to be a father. That was the reason he woke up in the mornings. It was what kept him going.

Angela walked over to the couch and sat down, and Evan took a seat in a chair facing her. Angela wasn't wearing any makeup and obviously didn't look like she usually did when he saw her.

Evan asked, "You feeling okay?"

Angela replied, "Just a little under the weather."

Evan responded, "Is there anything I can do for you?"

"Just keep doing what you've been doing. That's all I could ever ask for." she said.

Evan wasn't sure what that meant. He had no clue how much the things he had been doing meant to her. He wasn't aware of the change he had made in their lives.

Angela had closed her eyes and leaned her back on the chair. Evan wondered what she was thinking or whether she just felt that tired. As they sat there quietly, he felt awkward and wondered if he should just go outside and wait for Mason; but he knew he had a lot that needed to be said. He just wanted to lay it all out right then and there.

Angela opened her eyes and looked his way as she lifted her head.

He couldn't hold back any longer as he blurted out, "I have some things that I really need to tell you."

"Okay?" she replied.

Her demeanor gave him the impression that she didn't really didn't care very much for him. She didn't want him to think she was giving in to him just because of everything he had done for her and Mason. She felt as if she'd look weak and desperate, and she had not forgotten how desperate she had been when she was pregnant with Mason. Yet, it was impossible for her not to appreciate how easy things had been since Evan had been coming. She didn't understand how he was able to be there. She had an even harder time trying to figure out why he wanted to be there. *Why now?* That was the question she had been asking herself. Angela wanted to put up a wall, but it was getting harder and harder to do. Deep down inside she badly wanted to know what it was he had to say to her.

Evan continued the conversation, "They are things that should be said over dinner."

She replied, "Oh? Well, I guess that's okay."

"Yeah? Is next Friday okay?" he asked.

"Yes" she responded. She stood and said, "I'm going to go back and lie down."

Evan replied, "Oh sure, Go ahead. Again, I'm sorry for disturbing. I hope you feel better soon." She smiled, then turned around and walked to her bedroom. Evan stood and watched her walk away.

He started to sit back down when he heard the sound of the school bus. He walked to the door and opened it as Mason came running in with excitement as he always did when he knew Evan would be there. Every time he saw Mason, he was reminded of all that he had missed. He watched as Mason came nearer and felt happy that he was now a part of his life and …

another afternoon with his son was about to begin.

Confinement

Over the past couple of weeks, the mornings had felt as if they lasted forever. From the time he got home until he woke up, Evan stayed in his bedroom. He confined himself in that space in order to escape everything else in his world. Evan couldn't believe he was back where he felt chained to the wrong life. He was thankful for the time he had with Mason every day and was able to get a taste of what he wanted life to be like. Still, he wanted more.

He did all he could to avoid his grandfather and the tough conversation he would need to have with him. It was inevitable that he could only stay out of his sight so long. On the Saturday after the first week of being with his son, Evan walked out of his room to see if his grandfather was there. Evan didn't mean for his grandfather to see him; but as he looked down the staircase, he was standing there looking directly up at him.

"Heard you were a no show this week. Is that true?" he asked Evan.

Evan ignored him as he waked down the stairs and headed for the kitchen. His grandfather walked behind him and said

"Talk to me! Is that true? What's going on?"

"Yes, it's true. That's exactly what's going on." Evan said as he turned around to look his grandfather eye to eye. Evan continued, "I'll tell you what else is going on. I'm not going be who YOU want me to be. I hate that person."

His grandfather huffed, "You just keep digging yourself a hole, boy."

"No! I'm getting out of the hole I've been buried in my entire life." Evan responded.

"What are you exactly trying to say?" his grandfather asked.

Evan firmly announced, "I quit!"

Evan went back up to his room, gathered a few essentials and left the house. He headed for Raleigh to his apartment where most of his belongings had been left. He had needed to escape from his home once again and enjoyed being alone as he drove on Interstate-40. There were still decisions he had to make about the other job he was also not satisfied about. He had put a lot of energy into getting elected as state senator after a long campaign. Now he felt like that was nothing but wasted time. Evan realized he had another tough conversation ahead of him. The only way for him to feel free to be who he wanted to be was to resign from the senate seat. He knew that leaving two jobs in one day was a very unusual practice. Yet, Evan didn't view them as jobs anymore; they had become burdens to him.

After completely cleaning out his apartment, he began his journey back home. With his car filled with boxes full of his belongings, he had now left behind everything he didn't want to be. Back at home, as the days went by, Evan didn't feel the need to talk to anybody. In the mornings, when he went to the kitchen to get breakfast, he would just walk past his mother who sat at the kitchen table alone every day. One morning he woke up and made his way downstairs as usual. As he started by the table, he felt drawn to sit down with her. After making his breakfast, he pulled back a chair and sat across from his mother. She was surprised as she looked up from her crossword puzzle to see Evan sitting there.

"Hello." Evan said to her.

She smiled at him and that began a new daily ritual between the two of them. Every morning he ate breakfast and visited with his mother. He didn't reveal to her what he was doing, he knew he just couldn't yet. There were still so many things she didn't know about him. He hated keeping what had become such a big part of his life from her. Evan assured her that he had a "new job" he was focusing on. He couldn't wait for the day when everything would all make sense. When that would be, he had no clue.

Evan's mother never asked him of his whereabouts. She knew there was something worthwhile happening since he was leaving so many things behind.

Their relationship had improved so that they had been able to connect in ways they had not before. They could better relate when it was just the two of them without distractions. They had never had the chance to experience much one-on-one time ever before. After a couple of weeks of their everyday talks, Evan wanted to know about his mother personal life. He felt like he was understanding her better as a mother, but there was so much more to her life. There was no way Evan could understand the struggle of raising a child without a father. He wanted to hear that from someone who did, his mother. That would be a stepping stone to reconnecting with Angela. He knew if he was ever going to be in her life the way he wanted to be, he needed to know the kind of life she had been living.

The day finally came. After what seemed like the longest week yet, on Friday morning he went downstairs where his mother was sitting at the kitchen table as usual. She had a crossword puzzle in one hand and a cup of coffee in the other. She thought she saw something different about Evan as he moved with more pep in his step.

"Everything okay?" she asked.

He couldn't help smiling and replied, "Everything's great" as he poured his cereal into the bowl. His mother took her pencil off the top of her ear and looked back down at her puzzle.

"I do have something to ask you." he said.

"What is it?" she asked.

He took deep breath and asked, "What was the most challenging thing about raising me alone?"

She put her pencil down and sat up in her chair. She had not seen this question coming. She responded, "You know, there were so many challenges. The toughest times were when you weren't here with me. I had nobody to fill the void. There was nothing my dad could do to help. That's was the hardest."

Evans expression went from a smile to a much more serious look. He had never heard his mother be so honest and open before. Evan went back upstairs and sat in his room to wait for time to be with Mason. It seemed time crept slower than it ever had. Over the next couple of hours, Evan thought about what his mother had said. He tried to put it all in perspective as it related to

Angela's life. He wanted to do everything he could to help fill any void she had in her life.

The afternoon had finally arrived. Evan put on his daily outfit, Khakis and a collared shirt. He combed his hair the same way he did every day. His daily routine never changed. Everything on the outside seemed normal, but still he could barely contain himself. Evan went to his closet and took out his coat. He felt inside the pocket for the small box he had placed there several weeks ago. Evan was about to get ahead of himself, once again stuck inside of what was still a fantasy.

He went downstairs a little earlier than he usual. He was looking around for his mother when she appeared behind him.

"Right here." she said, with a laundry basket in her hands.

Evan said, "Oh, hey I'm-" "Heading out, I know" she said, as this was his daily pattern now. "Look I've got something big today and-"

"I understand" she said breaking him off again, "Do what you need to do. You'll look nice doing it." she said with a smile.

Evan smiled and kissed her forehead. He turned around and walked toward the front door. His daily half-hour drive was awaiting him, and so were all of his wildest dreams.

Friday afternoons were different. No homework meant there was more time spent out in the yard kicking the soccer ball. Evan realized that Mason needed some way to connect with other kids his age.

He asked Mason, "How would you like to play on a team?"

"With other kids? I don't know. Why can't I just keep playing with you?" Mason answered.

Evan replied, "You can always do that, but it would be good to make some friends too, you know?"

"Well, only if you coach." Mason said.

Coach? Evan thought as he pictured a group of uncontrollable kids running around everywhere. He then saw the look on Mason's face and knew he couldn't say no to that.

"Yeah, Okay sure. I'll do it." Evan said, as he remembered he had nothing better to do.

Mason had a big smile on his face. Seeing that made anything worth doing for Evan.

"Well it's starting to get dark, let's go inside." Evan said.

The sun had almost completely set as another afternoon was coming to an end. Evan had kept eyeing the road the entire time just waiting for Angela's car to appear. He had been waiting for what felt like an eternity. As they walked toward the house, headlights were shining on the driveway. Evan turned around to see the same car he saw every day.

"Mommy's home!" yelled Mason.

Evan stood back as Mason ran toward the car that was now parked. Angela opened the door as she was talking with someone on the phone. Mason wrapped his arms around her and hugged her waist. With the phone in one hand, she put her hands through his hair with the other. "I'll talk to you Monday" she said as she hung up the phone.

She put her phone in her pocket and bent down to hug her son. She then stood up, opened the back door of her car, and picked up her work bag along with a hand full of papers. She looked absolutely exhausted.

"Can I help you with anything?" Evan asked her.

"I've got it." She said, as she walked past him.

"*Well can I at least open the door? Or can she do that too.*" he thought to himself as he went up the front steps and held the door open for her. Angela walked through the door, pretending to pay no attention to Evan. She went over to the kitchen and dropped the stack of papers on the table and sat her bag down on the chair.

Evan asked, "So, how was your day?"

"Busy, very busy. How about you?" she asked.

Evan thought to himself for a moment, realizing that his life was now anything but busy. He still replied, "Oh yeah, same here."

As Angela walked over to the coat rack, Evan asked, "So, where do you want to eat tonight?"

"Tonight?" She asked, then said, "Oh yeah, tonight. It doesn't matter to me."

She gave the impression that she had almost forgotten that they would be going out for dinner. In reality, that was all she had thought about all week. "There was one thing I didn't think of" She said.

Evan asked, "What's that?" She replied, "There's nobody to watch Mason."

Evan quickly said, "No, no." thinking of the things he needed to say to her privately.

Angela held her arms up in the air, "I don't know what you want me to do."

"What about the neighbors?" Evan asked. Angela responded, "I don't know any of them well enough to do that."

Evan thought for a moment, and then asked, "What about your parents?"

Angela's eyes widened, "My parents? I don't know if that's a good idea."

Evan, didn't understand what she meant by this. All he knew was something had to be done in order for them to have dinner.

"Wasn't there a babysitter?" he asked.

Angela replied, "That's you. Remember? I cancelled on the other one."

"Look, please. Let's go to your parents' house. You can't avoid this any longer." Evan insisted.

What Evan was referring to avoiding was their dinner, but the only thing that came to Angela's mind was her parents.

Angela thought for a moment, "Okay." she said, "Let's go."

Angela called Mason, who had gone into another room.

As he came running back, he asked, "What's going on?"

"We're going to Grandma's." Angela told him.

Evan thought Mason would be excited to go to his Grandparents' home; but instead, he acted confused … as if he didn't know whether they should go there. They walked out of the door and Angela locked it behind them.

She told Evan, "Let's drive my car. The car seat is already in it."

They got into Angela's car with Evan sitting in the driver's seat. He backed out the driveway, and headed out of the neighborhood. As they made their way, everything was silent. Evan looked over to Angela and saw her sitting there straight faced and looking pale. Evan didn't know what had happened to Angela after mentioning her parents. All he knew was that there was something going on in her mind. He still couldn't piece the puzzle together.

"You know how to get there?" Angela asked, breaking the silence.

"I think I've got an idea." Evan said, trying not to sound too sure when in fact he knew exactly where.

He was surprised that Angela hadn't flooded him with more questions than she had. She hadn't had much to say since the encounter they had that night weeks before. As they neared her parents' neighborhood, Evan looked into the rear view mirror and saw that Mason was asleep. He glanced over to Angela again and saw her head leaning against the car window as she seemed to stare out at the dark surroundings. The silence made the short trip feel longer. Looking at her raised the tension and his nerves were once again on edge.

He turned into the small neighborhood just as he had a few weeks ago, this time from a different direction. Angela, still looking out of the window, saw the neighborhood and immediately faced forward. She sat up in her seat as in she thought, *this is actually happening.* Evan pulled the care into her parent' driveway and stopped the car. He looked over to Angela and asked, "Do you need a moment alone with them?" Angela nodded her head as she didn't know Evan had had an encounter with her parents. She reached her arm to the backseat to wake up Mason who had been exhausted from running around the yard all afternoon.

His eyes slowly opened, Angela said, "C'mon, Bud."

Angela opened the car door and helped him out of the car seat. She stood him up and held his hand as they walked towards the front porch. Evan sat in the car ... all he could do was watch and wait.

Mr. and Mrs. Sanders had just finished eating dinner. Mr. Sanders was in the kitchen doing dishes as his wife saw a reflection from outside.

"Are those headlights in our driveway?" she asked.

He responded, "Headlights? Can you tell who it is?"

"Honey, it looks like Angela's car." she told him.

"Oh stop that, you're just seeing things." Mr. Sanders assured her.

The doorbell then rang, and Mrs. Sanders looked at her husband. "I'll get it." he said.

He walked to the door and peeked out of the window seeing that the car looked familiar. He slowly opened the door and there they stood.

"My God." he said in shock.

"Who is it?" his wife said from the background.

She walked from behind him and was shocked to see her daughter and grandson standing there.

"Hey you guys." Angela said.

Her mother quickly opened up her arms to embrace her. Her father still stood there in disbelief. He looked down at Mason who was staring up at him and picked him up.

"Come on in you guys." her mother said to Angela.

"Well here's the thing." Angela told them.

They all heard the car door when it closed, and then they saw Evan walking around the front of the car. Not thinking he would get out, Angela looked at him and said to herself, *"What is he doing?"* Her parents were also not expecting to see him there. Still, it was all beginning to make sense to them. What Mrs. Sanders had hoped for by sending Evan to her had happened. Mr. Sanders looked at Evan standing there and then looked at his daughter and grandson. He hadn't seen the two of them in months. Knowing Evan was the reason for this visit, he gained immediately had a different feeling toward him.

Angela still thought that her parents hadn't seen Evan in years. She had no idea that he was the reason she was standing there with them.

"You remember Evan, right?" Angela asked.

"We do… I think we do." Her mother said as she looked at her husband.

Angela asked them, "Could Mason stay with you all for a little while long enough for us to go to dinner?"

"Sure! Go ahead." Mr. Sanders said to her.

Angela had not expected the visit to go so smoothly, but she didn't question it. She thanked her parents and turned to walk to the car where Evan was waiting. He opened the door for her, and she got in. Evan turned around to see her mother and Mason make their way inside. Mr. Sanders remained still as he and Evan made eye-to-eye contact. Mr. Sanders gave Evan a nod as he opened the front door to go back inside.

Evan, back on the driver's side, opened the car door and looked over at Angela. "Everything okay?" he asked.

"Just surprised, I guess. I don't know." Angela responded.

Not only was Angela surprised, she was mostly confused at the reaction her parents had at seeing Evan there. Everything that had been happening still wasn't adding up to her. Angela had so much she needed to know She figured Evan would be the one with all the answers, but …

it was up to her to ask.

The Reservation

It was well past 6 PM as Evan turned onto the street and drove toward the busier section of town. Neither of them said anything as they continued toward their destination.

Evan broke the silence. "Getting a little hungry. How about you?" Evan asked, just to make conversation.

Angela replied, "Most definitely so."

She had her elbow leaning against the passenger door with her hand on her head and was staring out of the window like she had never been in that part of town before. It was as if she was looking for something, but in reality, she was just looking away from someone. Evan was a little nervous ... this was the dinner with Angela that he had been looking forward to all week. As they approached the downtown area, the street lights lit the entire place making it a beautiful sight. Evan noticed all the families together on the sidewalks and the couples holding hands. That's what he pictured with Angela; but judging from her demeanor so far, it seemed what he wished for was becoming a long shot.

Evan didn't even attempt to say anything else in the car. He continued to drive slowly as he turned onto Turnage Street. At the end of the street, he pulled into a parking lot that was beside a building the two of them had seen many times before. Angela turned her head forward to see the sign that read, *The Abbey*. She sat gazing at the sign and then looked over to see that Evan was already out of the car. Suddenly the passenger door opened, and Evan was standing there with his hand held out for her. Angela realized her mind was somewhere else entirely. She had not even noticed when he had gotten out of the car. She took Evan's hand and stood up out of the car and shivered a little when she felt the chilly air on her skin.

"You cold?" he asked.

She avoided looking directly at Evan's eyes, knowing that was all it would take for her to give in to him.

"I'm fine for now." Angela replied as she walked by Evan's side.

The two of them made their way to the front door of the restaurant. Evan held the front door open for her and two other people who were behind them. Angela stood aside and waited for Evan.

As he came in, she asked him the question that was on her mind, "Are you actually a different person or are you just showing off?"

"A little of both." he said with a smile.

They walked over to the hostess stand and waited behind the two people for whom Evan had held the door. Angela noticed the sign that read, *Wait time: 45 Minutes.* She remembered that Evan was not one for wanting to wait.

"Guess I shouldn't have been showing off." he whispered to Angela, trying to lighten up her mood. It was all she could do to keep from smiling.

"Next." called the hostess.

Evan walked up to the stand and said, "Reservation for Stevenson."

"Okay Mr. Stevenson, follow me." said the hostess.

"Angela looked toward Evan and said, "Reservations? You've thought all this through."

Evan replied, "Yes, I have."

They continued to follow the hostess to a table near the back of the restaurant. In Evans eyes, there was a spotlight on the small table straight ahead of them. He almost felt like it had their names written on it.

The hostess held out her arm to the table, "Someone will be right with y'all. Enjoy."

Evan took a deep breath as he walked to the other side of the table to pull out the chair for Angela. She sat down and he did the same. Evan realized he would have to be the one to start the conversation. He knew, if he didn't, it would be a quiet evening.

He pointed over toward a random booth and said, "I think that's where we used to always sit."

As Angela looked at it, she thought, *No it's not.* She remembered exactly where it was. Instead of saying it that way, she sarcastically replied, "Great memory you have there."

Evan didn't want to have to turn things into a serious conversation at this point. He just hoped throughout the evening his actions would speak for everything he wanted to say to her. What he didn't know was that Angela had other plans. She wasn't there for small talk. She was there to get a better understanding of everything that had transpired in the past few days in her life. "So Mason seems pretty excited for our first practice tomorrow." Evan said.

Angela responded, "Yeah…yeah that's great."

Evan continued, "I think it'll be a fun .."

Angela stopped him, "Evan…How on earth is it that you are sitting here with me tonight?"

"I'm sorry?" he asked, startled at what she had just asked.

"How did you find me?" she asked.

Evan sat back in his chair. He knew that question would eventually be asked, but he hadn't expected it so soon and had no clue how to begin answering it right then.

"It's really a long story." he said. "Well, I'm here to listen to it." she responded.

Before Evan could begin to answer, the waiter came to the table at the worst time possible.

"Can I get y'all something to drink?" he asked.

"Just water." Evan replied. "Same for me." Angela said.

As the waiter walked away, Evan continued. "I've just had a different view of life and …"

"Here are your waters." the waiter said as he came back to their table. "Are y'all ready to order?" "Don't think so." Evan said as he was becoming annoyed.

"Well then. Let me know when." said the waiter as he walked away.

Evan took a deep breath and continued, "I have a lot of regrets, you know?"

"Evan, answer my question." Angela said, "How did you find me?"

"Okay, okay. I was led to your parents' house. I had been looking for you. All they could tell me was the name of your neighborhood." He continued, "One thing led to another ... and well, here I am." He said with a hint of laughter.

He looked across the table to see that Angela not even close to laughing. It all started to come together for her. Her focus was on her parents. She wondered if they had gotten him to do all of this just to be in her life again. She had thought about all the events in her life that had led to this. She remembered having to leave school to move back in with her parents and raise her son. She remembered being so young and having to sacrifice her dreams. She remembered how far she had come since she had been on her own ... and she knew she didn't want go back.

"Angela?" Evan asked from across the table. Before she could respond, the waiter was at the table with their dinner.

During their meal Angela didn't have much to say. An awkward silence that Evan had feared was getting to him. Any comment he made was acknowledged with a nod of her head or brief answer. It was hard for her to think of anything to say when her mind was only focused on the negative impact he had on her life in the past. She appreciated everything Evan had done for Mason and her but couldn't convince herself that he was being genuine. She wondered if all the recent acts of kindness that had brought them happiness again was just a big setup. Fortunately, the waiter came with the check just as they had finished the meal. Evan decided to pay at the counter rather than sit at the table in an uncomfortable silence while they waited for him to bring back his change. Evan stood up to leave, and as he did Angela pushed her chair back. He rushed around the table to be courteous in assisting her. She walked a few steps ahead of him as they left the restaurant.

The dinner date hadn't turned out the way he had hoped. He had looked forward to a warm conversation with him having opportunity to explain everything to her. The worst part was that they had hardly said anything. Maybe it just wasn't the right time ... maybe it would never be the right time. As they walked outside, Evan still hoped something good would come from their time together.

Angela, still walking ahead of him, walked faster as they went in the parking lot.

"I'll drive." she said as they neared her car.

Evan picked up his pace to the car thinking that Angela might not have any problem leaving him there. She was already in the driver's seat as he opened the other door and sat down in the passenger seat. She started the car and pulled out of the parking lot onto the downtown street. He looked over at Angela who was staring straight ahead and saying nothing as if Evan wasn't even there. During the drive back toward Angela's parents' house, Evan was the one staring out the window. He stared into the darkness with no clue as to what would come next in his life. Evan now wondered if he had left everything behind to take a chance on something that never would be … his desire to have the kind of life he had never experienced … with a real a family. That dream was all he had focused on. He just couldn't let it end like this.

Not a word had been spoken from the restaurant until the time she drove the car into the neighborhood where her parents lived. She drove quickly down their street and into their driveway. She got out of the car quickly. "Just stay here." she told Evan as the door was shutting.

He watched her walk up the steps of the front porch and knock on the door. He could see Mason and her mother when the door opened.

"Come in!" said her Mother with a smile.

Angela had spent the entire ride from the restaurant thinking of what to say when she got there … but in that moment, she had nothing. This was the last place she wanted to be right now. She didn't even seem to care about the smile on her son's face or on her mother's.

"We really need to get going. It's getting late." Angela said to her.

Her mother replied, "Oh, well okay. Mason, go get your coat."

As Mason ran into the other room, her mother looked at her and asked, "So, how did it go tonight?"

Angela said, "I don't know. I'm sure you would have wanted it go really well, wouldn't you?"

Mrs. Sanders, confused at Angela's response, said, "Well, of course."

Mason came running back to the door. Angela told him, "Go get in the car. I'll be there in a second."

Mason walked outside and toward the car, and Mrs. Sanders shut the door behind him.

She looked closely at Angela and asked, "What's the matter with you?"

"You think you can just send him over out of nowhere to come in my life again?" Angela asked. Her mother responded, "Look, he came to us. He was looking for you ... just like we have been." Well, here I am." Angela said, "You got what you wanted. Now I really need to go."

Her mother watched as Angela opened the door and walked out without another word. She closed it shut not knowing the next time she would see her or her grandson. Mrs. Sanders could not understand what was causing the distance between her and Angela. She didn't know that it really had nothing to do with them and there was nothing she could do about it.

As Angela walked to the car, she felt a sense of guilt. She was walking away like she had so many times before without even knowing why. As she got closer to the car, she could hear the sound of Evan and Mason laughing. When she opened the door the laughter came to a stop as they saw that she was noticeably upset. Throughout the entire drive, Mason talked about what he did at his grandparents' house in explicit detail. Hearing him joyously talk nonstop, Angela's feeling of guilt multiplied.

The three of them arrived back at Angela's neighborhood. Everything looked peaceful and serene as they rode past the *Cedar Hill* sign that was lit up in the night. Nearing the cul-de-sac, they turned right into Angela's driveway. Evan was reminded when he saw his car that he was going to have a late drive home.

They got out of the car and Angela said to Evan, "Wait here."

She held Mason's hand as they walked to the front door. Mason turned around and said to Evan, "See ya tomorrow!" Evan smiled and waved to him.

Evan stood there waiting for Angela as she had told him to do. He wasn't at all sure of what she had in mind. He was confused as to what had caused the night to become so disastrous.

After a few minutes, Angela came out of the house. Evan was leaning against his car with his breath visible in the cold air.

"Evan." She said, getting his attention, "We need to talk."

He looked up from his phone and began to walk toward her.

"I believe everything will be better staying like they have been." she said.

As he got closer to her, he replied, "Do you really believe that? Or do you just want to think that?" Angela didn't sound too convincing as she replied, "I just know. Okay?"

Evan took a few steps back, not having enough energy to argue back.

He replied, "If that's what you want, then by all means."

As he started walking away, Angela said, "I think there's someone who will be expecting you back here tomorrow."

Evan quickly turned around, and said, "Then you better believe I will be here."

There was nothing left to say as Evan got in his car and Angela watched his headlights get smaller as he backed out of the driveway. He drove off going toward his mother's house. He would go there where he would try to forget the very confusing night. Angela went back inside to try to do the same thing. She was left with so many questions that she couldn't answer for herself. She still had so much she didn't know, and her selfish ways continued to block out any hope of getting the answers.

Evan felt physically and mentally exhausted. He blasted his radio at high volume trying to stay awake as he drove back home. When he turned into the neighborhood, he turned his radio down. He slowly pulled into the driveway that circled around the front yard. Evan carefully walked up the front steps and reached for his house key. He gently unlocked the door and slowly opened it to the dark and quiet house. After shutting and locking the door he walked directly up the stairs and into his bedroom. He immediately fell back on his bed feeling as if he had nothing left in him anymore.

Evan closed his eyes, hoping for a peaceful moment. In that moment he saw himself sitting in the cabin overlooking the still water with Linwood sitting beside him. He knew that he could use another talk with his Grandfather Linwood. He immediately sat up and realized that now he had the opportunity to do so. He reached in the small pocket and grabbed the slip of paper with the number Linwood had given him several weeks ago. Evan couldn't believe he had completely forgotten about that phone number. He looked over at the clock beside his bed. It was *11:38 p.m.* Evan thought that Linwood was probably closer to his waking hour than his bedtime hour. He grabbed his phone and dialed in the number that was on the paper. As it rang on the other end, he was hoping that Linwood would answer it. After ringing several times, Linwood's machine picked up.

From the heart, Evan said, "Hey Grandad. It's me, Evan. I know it's very late, but I'm so sorry I haven't called. Over the past weeks so much has happened that I can't wait to tell you about. I've missed you."

Evan slowly put down the phone and stared at the paper. He felt deep regret for missing out on much needed conversation in the past weeks. He took off his coat and turned out his lamp. He knew needed to try and get some rest so he could get an early start to the next day. As he shut his eyes, sleep came quickly. It took him back to that place where his uncertainty went away ... the place where all of life's questions were answered ... somewhere that wasn't a fantasy, but a place he had been before. It was where he always wanted to be.

Early the next morning, while most people where in the middle of their sleep, Linwood was about to start another day. He didn't know what he'd do if there wasn't a job waiting to be done when he woke up. With that on his mind, eased out of bed like he always did and went through his usual morning routine. Linwood walked into the kitchen from his bedroom and noticed the light blinking on the house phone machine. He turned on the kitchen light and walked toward it. He thought it could be the milk company calling him about another pickup from his farm. Linwood had almost given up hope on hearing back from Evan after the days of waiting had turned into weeks. He pressed the *Play Message* button, and the voicemail that Evan had sent began to play out loud.

Linwood was in complete shock as he hadn't expected to hear Evan's voice. He replayed it several times to hear the number it was from. He tore off a small part of a sheet of paper and grabbed a pen to write the number down. Linwood placed it in his shirt pocket knowing he'd call it back as soon as he could. He went outside into the cold and dark morning ...

another day of work was ahead of him.

Change of Plans

Evan woke up to the unpleasant sound of his alarm on that Saturday morning. It was the last sound he wanted to hear on the weekend, and he was tempted to go back to sleep. However, he knew who was expecting him and that was all he needed to get him up and going. He wasn't sure how things would go today. After the way last night ended, he wasn't one hundred percent sure that time with Mason would even be possible. He looked at his phone. It read *7:03 a.m.* Evan pushed the covers aside to get up. He was taking on something new, which he found himself doing quite often now. He was stepping out of his comfort zone for the good of someone else ... his son. Taking on the responsibility of not just one kid but several others as a coach for the winter youth soccer team was something he had never imagined himself doing.

When Evan went out of the house, the sun was beginning to shine brightly. Afraid he would be late, Evan hurried to his car, got in and started it. He was once again back on the road. Evan knew the miles had been adding up in all his going back forth. He felt as if he could now make the drive to Angela's house with his eyes closed. The drive went quickly, and he was soon parking on the side of the street at Angela's house. He walked up to the front door like he had done many times before.

Evan knocked on the door, and Angela opened it immediately.

Without any greeting, Angela said, "You'll have to go in there and talk to Mason. He doesn't want to go."

Evan wondered what had happened. He went to Mason's room and found him sitting on his bed in tears.

"What's wrong, buddy?" Evan asked, as he knelt down beside his bed.

Through his tears, Mason responded, "I can't do it."

"Can't do what?" Evan asked.

"I can't be with those other kids. I'm not like them. They're gonna hate me." Mason said as tears rolled down his face.

"Look at me." Evan said, "Look me in the eyes." Mason slowly lifted his head to hear Evan say, "Don't you ever think that. They will love you, because you're… you're awesome … in every single way."

Angela stood in the hallway eavesdropping on what Evan had said to Mason. She could never emotionally connect with her son. The only person who had been able to get close to him was Evan. As she heard what he said, she realized she had made the right choice by allowing Evan in her son's life. She also wondered if she had been making the wrong one by keeping him out of her own.

Evan wiped Mason's tears off his face and said, "Now come on, let's go have fun."

Mason's feelings immediately changed as Evan had completely inspired him … as he always did. There was nobody he looked up to more than he did Evan. He was his best friend. Angela hurried back into the living room, pretending she hadn't heard anything that was said in Mason's room.

Evan walked in with Mason following him. "Alright, we're doing this!" Evan shouted. Angela gave a soft smile and said, "Have fun, you guys."

Mason walked out the front door with Evan, and got into his car. As Evan got in, he looked into the rear view mirror to see a sight he never imagined seeing. He saw his son sitting there in the car seat looking out of the window. The more he looked at him, the more he could see himself.

After driving a few minutes, Evan's phone began to buzz as it was sitting in the cup holder. He picked it up and glanced at the screen to see a number that he didn't recognize. He swiped his finger on the screen to answer it. "Evan Stevenson" he answered. The voice on the phone replied, "Evan, this is James from the farm. You need to come to the county hospital, now."

"James? What's going on? How'd you-" Evan responded.

"Look, there's no time for questions. It's Mr. Linwood." James said.

"My God." Evan softly said as he hung up the phone.

Evan pulled off the side of the road and immediately turned around. His foot pressed down on accelerator and the car speeded up considerably.

"What's going on?" Mason asked from the backseat. Evan's mind was completely racing. Not wanting to say too much, he replied, "We were just going the wrong direction."

The car continued to speed towards the hospital, that was closer to Evan's house than Angela's. They came to the busy part of town and turned into the busy hospital parking lot.

Seeing the large building, Mason again asked, "What's going on? Where are we?"

"I'll tell you in a minute." Evan replied.

After minutes of looking, he found a parking spot and got out of the car. He opened Mason's door and helped him out.

Bending down on one knee, he said, "Look, I have to visit someone that I love. This is very important. I promise I'll make it up to you."

Mason simply replied, "Okay."

Evan took Mason's hand in his as they walked through the parking lot toward the main entrance. Before going inside, Evan pulled out his phone and sent Angela a message explaining the entire situation. After walking through the automatic door, they walked to the front desk.

"How can I help you?" The lady at the desk asked.

"Yes, I'm here to see Linwood Johnson." Evan frantically said.

"Okay sir. Calm down and sign this." she said.

After signing the visitor form, she handed him a slip of paper with the room number on it. They got into the elevator and headed up to the fourth floor. Evan's heart was pounding as the elevator door opened up. They got off and walked in the busy hallway looking right to left for room 21A. They found it at the end of the hallway on the left. Evan knocked on the door, then slowly opened it. They walked into the quiet room where Evan saw Linwood lying there in the hospital bed with his eyes closed. There was a machine beeping quietly and tubes and cords were all over the place. Evan looked over across the bed where he saw James sitting in a chair in the corner of the room.

Like Linwood, his eyes were closed too.

The sound of Evan clearing his throat woke James up from his light sleep. As his eyes slowly opened, he said, "Oh, you're here. About time."

James stood up and told Evan, "Come with me."

They walked out into the hallway with Mason still holding Evans's hand.

Before Evan could ask anything, James said, "He had a heart attack. Everything happened so fast. He kept pointing to his shirt pocket and well, this was in there."

James pulled out the small piece of paper with Evan's number written on it. "So then I called you." he said.

Evan felt himself filling with grief as he wished there was something he could've done. James went back in the room, and Evan followed him. James walked over to the side of Linwood's bed and softly tapped on his shoulder.

He said, "Sir, you have a visitor."

Linwood's eyes slowly opened and grew wide as he saw Evan standing there.

James told Evan, "I'll give you guys a moment alone."

Evan looked down at Mason and said, "Do you want to go with Mr. James?"

He knew there was so much he needed to say to Linwood. He wasn't comfortable letting Mason hear it. Evan trusted James as he watched Mason walk out of the door with him.

"You've been busy, I can see." Linwood said.

Evan turned around and replied, "Very. So much has happened, all thanks to you."

"Me? How so?" Linwood asked.

Evan said, "There was a lot that happened before in my life that I kept private. That boy right there, that's my son." He continued, "You inspired me to find him ... and her."

Linwood was more surprised to hear he inspired Evan than to find out he had a son. As he laid there, his heart filled with joy.

He asked Evan, "Her? Where is she." Evan replied, "Things are still difficult right now for her...and for me."

"The best things in life take time. In the beginning they may look lifeless, then sprouts come and turn into something beautiful. Just give it some time to grow ... give yourself some time to grow." Linwood softly said.

Tears began to build up in Evan's eyes as Linwood's powerful words had spoken to him once again. He had missed his advice badly and needed to hear it now more than ever. Linwood slowly reached his hand out for Evan to shake. Instead, Evan bent over and hugged him as he helplessly laid there. After several minutes spent catching up with each other, there was a knock on the door. Evan turned around to see Mason walking in with a soda in his hand.

James walked in behind him and said, "That boy is already pulling money out of my pocket."

"I finally learned about the drink machines!" Mason said as he walked up to Evan.

"That's good, bud." Evan said as he grinned from ear-to-ear. He knelt down and told Mason, "I've got someone I want you to meet."

Evan turned around to look at Linwood then guided Mason over to the side his bed.

"This is Linwood. He's my best friend." he told Mason.

Tears began to stream down Linwood's face. So many emotions came to him as he saw his grandson and great-grandson in front of him. He realized this was the most family he'd seen in the same room in a long time. Not knowing how much time he had left, he couldn't ask for anything better.

"Hello." Mason said to him.

Linwood touched Mason's arm gently and said, "You're in good hands."

There was a swift knock on the door. "Nurse." said the voice from the outside.

"Well, I need to get Mason home, but I'll be back." Evan said.

Linwood held his hand out to Evan and just looked up at him ... no words were necessary. As Evan shook his hand and noticed that his grip was not nearly as strong as when he shook it last. As Evan let go, he gave a little wave and then walked toward the door. Mason took Evan's hand and then turned around to look back at the man lying in the hospital bed.

Linwood gave a weak smile and slowly waved his hand to him as they left the room.

Angela had seen Evan's message and wasn't sure what to do. A part of her was saying to just stay there at home, but there was something also urging her to go. She tried to call Evan, but he didn't pick up. She sat for a while wondering which feeling to follow and then thought *why not?* Angela kept telling herself, "I'll just go pick up Mason, that's all. Right?" She didn't know how to answer her own question. After pondering a few more minutes, she decided to make the trip to the hospital where she *thought* Evan and Mason were.

Angela was in somewhat of a hurry as she wasn't at all sure of what was going on. After pulling into the busy hospital parking lot, she pulled out her phone and attempted to call Evan again. Still there was no answer. Angela walked through the main entrance and to the front desk. Looking back at the message Evan had sent her to remember Evan's grandfather's name.

The lady at the desk greeted her, "Hello ma'am, how may I help you?"

Angela replied, "Hi, I'm here looking for a Linwood."

The lady looked on her computer and responded, "We have a Linwood Johnson on the fourth floor. Is that it?"

Angela didn't have any idea about the last name, but she thought there couldn't possibly be another Linwood in the hospital. After signing her name on the visitor sheet, she made her way to the elevator. As the door slid open on the fourth floor, she walked out and down the hall looking for the room number. She approached the end of the hallway where she saw it, Room 21A. As Angela neared the door, she paused for a second, took a deep breath and knocked on the door twice, then pushed it slightly open.

"Hello?" she said as she entered the room.

James peeked his head around the corner and didn't recognize her face. "Yes ma'am, you a nurse?"

She softly laughed and replied, "Oh no, I'm looking for Evan Stevenson. This must be the wrong room."

Linwood heard her mention Evan's name and hoped that it was the woman Evan had told him about.

Before James could say anything, Linwood's weak voice from farther in the room said, "Come in."

James moved aside as Angela went into the room where she saw an older man lying in the hospital bed.

"Do you know Evan?" she asked.

Linwood replied, "He's my grandson. I'm guessing you know him too."

"You must be Linwood." she said. "Did he and a small boy come here?"

"They just left not too long ago." Linwood said.

"Oh, well … I'm sorry to bother. I'll get going." she said.

As she was heading to the door, Linwood said to her, "You must be Angela."

She turned around, surprised that he knew her name. "I am." she responded.

"Look." he said, "I wish I could have known Evan longer than I have. However, I've known him long enough to see a change in him."

Angela slowly walked closer, "A change?"

"He needs you." Linwood said.

"I'm sorry?" She replied with a questioned look on her face.

"He needs you to keep that change going for him. I'm not sure if I'll be able to do so much longer." he said.

She responded, "Oh, don't say that."

"Ja-James." Linwood said as his hands began to tremble.

"Sir?" James said as he quickly stood up from his chair.

"Doctor." Linwood said, struggling. "Help."

Angela took several steps back as James ran out into the hallway and yelled for a doctor. She couldn't believe the situation she had gotten herself into. As she looked back toward Linwood's direction, she heard the heart monitors high pitch beep. Angela looked on the screen to see a flat line running across the screen, and she saw Linwood's eyes slowly beginning to shut.

As many people began to rush into the room, Angela was completely overwhelmed with emotion. She had never been in a situation like that. She looked over to James who was standing by the door looking like he was in complete shock. Tears began to roll down her face as she heard one of the doctors say, "He's gone." She had known it before anyone else … before the person who meant the most to Linwood. Angela had no idea how she would begin to tell Evan but knew she had no choice but to do so.

As she slowly walked out of the room, she saw the tears flowing down James' face. He had no clue what to do. Linwood was the reason for so much in his life. With him now gone, he had no idea where to go or what to do. Angela didn't know anything about James' association with Linwood, but she saw that he was distraught.

She walked to his side and put her hand on his shoulder and said, "You won't go through this alone."

If James had reacted this way, she couldn't even begin to imagine how Evan would handle this.

As Angela drove back home, what had happened in the hospital room played over and over in her head. She felt her phone buzzing in her pocket didn't answer it. She knew it was probably Evan wondering where she was. It was past lunchtime when she got back to her neighborhood. She knew what a difficult conversation was coming. She thought about what Linwood had told her...how she needed to keep the change alive in Evan. She could not help but remember who Evan had been when he abandoned her in her most desperate time. That memory stood in the way of her being able to believe the way he now seemed to live his life was genuine. She had thought there was no way he would ever change, but had he?

Angela pushed her questioning thoughts aside as she drove into her driveway. Evan and Mason were in the front yard with the soccer ball as usual. She turned her car off and glanced at her phone. The calls had been from Evan just as she suspected. She got out of her car to the sound of Mason calling her name, but she didn't respond. Her mind was on Evan. She saw him standing there with no clue about where she had been nor what she was about to tell him.

Mason's voice cleared her mind, but she heard herself say, "Evan, can we talk."

The three of them went inside together. Mason's focus immediately switched to the television, so the two of them went out to the front porch.

As she shut the door, Evan was quick to ask, "So what's going on? I tried to call you."

Angela walked over to the one of the chairs and sat down. Evan followed her and sat in the other one.

"I went to the hospital, thinking you were there." she said.

Evan was surprised to hear that. He said, "You did? I'm sorry you drove all that way and had to turn around and come right back."

"Well, here's the thing. I didn't turn around. I went in." Angela said as lowered her head to avoid his eyes.

"Angela?" Evan asked, knowing something was wrong.

"I saw your grandfather." she said. "I saw everything … more than I ever wanted to see."

Evan was confused, and asked, "More than you wanted to see? What are you saying?" By this time, the tears had built up in Angela's eyes and began to flow down her cheeks.

"Evan, he's gone." she told him.

Evan sat there … staring off into space … not saying a word. It was as if what she had just told her went in one ear and out the other. Angela reached over tapped his shoulder, and he looked at her.

"Evan!" she said. At the sound of her voice, Evan's head began to shake and uncontrollable emotions took over.

"No! No! There's no way." he said, "It can't be.."

"I'm sorry, Evan. I was there. I saw everything." Angela told him.

Evan looked into her eyes and saw complete despair. It was then that he understood what was happening. Reality set in harder than he could have ever imagined. He was at loss. After a rollercoaster of emotions for the past months, he had reached an all-time low. As he sat there in despair, Angela placed her hand on his. There was nothing else she knew to say in that moment. Reaching out and touching his hand spoke volumes about everything she truly felt for him.

The minutes turned into hours, and then hours turned into days of nothing but grief and regret for Evan. The world was moving, but he felt it had left him behind. It was like his heart stood still as he replayed over and over in his mind the last few minutes he had with Linwood in the hospital. He spent his time alone in his bedroom away from everything else in the world. He kept his sadness bottled up until the time came when he had to face others.

It was day of Linwood's funeral. He went to his closet and took out his black suit. In his past lifestyle, he had worn that suit quite often. He took his time dressing as if trying to delay going where he had to go. When he went downstairs, just before walking out the door his mother gave him a hug. She said nothing, as she knew no words that would ease his sorrow. There was nothing she could do to make it easier. There was nothing anyone could do.

He walked outside to his car. Even the atmosphere was sad, he thought, as he looked up at the overcast morning sky. He got into his car and headed out to make the drive to the small church that was near the farm. The entire ride there was solemn. His mind was blank as he took in the scenery that he had so badly missed. As he approached the small church, he saw that cars had filled the front lawn and all along the sides of the road. Evan found a place to park, got out and began walking toward the front steps of the church. He stopped to clear his throat and try to swallow the lump that he felt there. Before walking through the doors, he was given a bulletin with a picture of his grandfather on the front. He paused to take a long look at it before he entered the church. The entire sanctuary was filled with people cramped from left to right. There was an open seat in the front row, but he still sat in the very back. Evan had never been comfortable in a church setting. He felt like he didn't belong. Other than James and the other men he had seen one day working at the farm, he had never seen any of the people there unless some of the men who were at the Mini Mart the day he met Linwood was in the crowd.

The service lasted nearly an hour. The musicians began to play and the pallbearers carried the casket down the aisle to go out of the church. James, who was one of them, noticed Evan standing in the last row. As everyone crowded out of the church, Evan was one of the last to leave. James was outside waiting for him, and he approached Evan as he walked down the front steps.

"Evan." James said, "Can I talk to you for a second?"

"Yeah, sure." Evan replied.

Evan followed James as he walked away from the crowd of people to the side of the church. "What's going on?" Evan asked.

"Evan, you're on Mr. Johnson's will." James replied.

Evan responded, "His will? You mean?"

"Yes, the land, the farm, Your name's on it."

James said, "I just wanted to say that I appreciate you coming today. He'd want you here. I know it."

Evan put his head down, trying to hide his emotions.

He replied, "It was my pleasure."

James continued, "I also wanted to tell you that I'm moving off to get work with somewhere else. There's not much opportunity for a guy like myself around here."

Evan was concerned at James plan so he asked, "What about the farm?"

James replied, "I mean come on, it's all over now. I talked to a lawyer. He said he'd get it all straightened out. Looks like you'll be set after selling all this."

"But it doesn't have to be over" Evan said.

"What? What do you mean?" James asked.

Evan thought about the uncertainty of what his next move would be in life. All he knew was that he needed something ... anything. He knew that money wouldn't be the solution.

Evan looked directly into James' eyes and responded, "I can help you run it."

James couldn't help himself. He began to sarcastically laugh until he saw the serious look on Evan's face.

"You serious? I mean, let's be real here." James said.

"Come on, James. Between you, me, and those other guys that you know, we can do it." Evan insisted.

"You're crazy. There's no way." James told Evan.

"Please, let's try it." Evan desperately said, "We can't just abandon this. We'll figure this thing out; and if we don't, you can go. He didn't put my name on this farm just so I could give it up." James was very skeptical of this idea. He didn't have any confidence it would work out, but he felt he owed this to Evan ... for Mr. Johnson's sake.

"Okay." James said. "Be at the farm by 4:00 this afternoon. James shook Evan's hand as he replied ...

If you wanna learn, we'll learn ... let's do it!"

Continuation

The conversation with James ended, and Evan made the walk back to his car parked on the side of the street. As Evan got into his car, he looked at the time and realized he had several hours to spare. It was just past lunch time. He knew his options were limited to only one place in the area. He slowly made his way onto the road and passed by the churchyard where the crowd lingered as he drove toward the Maybree Mini Mart.

He noticed the store was almost empty. He knew most people in the town had been at the church. He pulled beside a gas pump and made his way inside. Flashbacks hit him hard … the smell … the sound of the brass bell ringing when the door opened. He walked to the t back of the store where the same man he had seen weeks before came from the kitchen.

"Hey, it's you. Didn't think you'd last any more than a day around here." the worker said.

"I'd be lying if I said I didn't think the same thing. What are your specials today? "Evan asked. "Don't have any today. It's just what's on the menu." he said.

"Just give me a burger." Evan said.

Evan walked over to the refrigerated area and pulled out a bottle of Coca-Cola and placed it on the counter. He then pulled out his wallet and slid a twenty across the counter.

"That all for you today?" The worker asked.

"Should do it." Evan said, as he picked up his bag and headed out of the store.

After pumping gas in his car, he knew exactly where he wanted to go. He headed out of the gas station and onto the road in the direction of what looked like a ghost town. As he drove, Evan thought about the reality of being on his own now in a new environment. This time as he drove toward the farm, there wasn't anyone to follow. He passed by the church where a few people still lingered. He saw Johnson Road ahead. As he turned onto the road, a feeling of comfort and peace came over him. It was the feeling he had felt before ... and desperately needed to feel at that moment.

Evan turned onto the dirt driveway and stopped the car. He opened up his car door to see all the many things that his grandfather had left behind. He took a long look at his surroundings, not having a clue that it would be the most difficult task he had ever faced. With his bag of food in his hand, he walked up to the side door of the house. He tried to turn the doorknob but the door was locked. He bent down to the most obvious place a spare key would be found it there. After unlocking the door, he walked inside the dark and cold house. Though he had only been there a few times, it held fond memories for him. Evan was emotional as he began to walk through the house and reminisced about the precious moments he had with his grandfather there.

After finishing his meal at the small table, he stood up and looked into the mirror that had once revealed everything to him. It was the same mirror where he had once seen Linwood's reflection alongside him. Now he only saw himself still in the suit and tie he had chosen to wear to the funeral. He looked over to Linwood's closed bedroom door. He slowly approached it and reached for the doorknob. He opened the door to the dark room and walked over to Linwood's night stand where he picked up the old picture of a bride and groom. He sat on the edge of Linwood's bed and studied the picture. After placing the picture back, he opened up the drawer to find reading glasses and several of his grandfather's books.

Evan stood up and went to the closet that was straight ahead. He slid the door open. In it was an entire rack of work shirts and pants taking up the entire closet. He reached for a shirt and pair of pants thinking that he would wear them when he worked on the farm. After changing in the bathroom, he walked back toward the closet and saw a pair of rubber boots sitting there. They were a little tight but were a better option than his dress shoes. With them in hand, he walked out of the house. He sat down on the bench outside beside the door. He felt closer to Linwood than ever before. He just wished his grandfather were there with him.

As he was squeezing the boots on, an old pickup truck pulled into the driveway. James got out of the driver's seat and was followed by three other men.

"Looks like you made a trip into somebody's closet." James said.

Evan replied, "Thought it was better than the suit and tie."

"It is. You're lookin' like a real farmer now, I'll tell ya." James responded.

James then turned to the other guys he had brought with him to help work. "Fellas" he said, "This is Mr. Johnson's grandson, Evan. It was his idea to keep this thing going, so you can thank him for having a job."

Evan shook the hands of each of the men as James introduced them.

"Now the only way we're gonna make this work is if we do it together." James said. They all nodded their heads in agreement, and James said, "Well, let's begin by starting, fellas."

As the three men split into different directions, James looked at Evan and said, "Follow me, let me introduce you to a few things. We still have half an hour before milking time."

They walked toward the biggest building on the farm. Evan followed James as they approached a building made of cinder blocks that were painted white.

Before walking in the front door, James said to Evan, "This right here is the dairy barn where all the magic happens."

James went through the narrow door first with Evan close behind him. As they entered, the high ceiling captured Evan's attention. He had never seen anything like this before. James pointed out the two steps, on both the left and right side, that led up to a higher platform.

"This is where the cows stand." James said as he walked up the stairs. "They come from the back area here through these sliding doors, and we have five slots where they stand while being milked."

Evan nodded his head to everything James said as he tried to picture all of this happening.

James continued, "The same exact thing goes for that side over there." He started down the stairs and toward the middle alleyway. "Right here we'll have myself, and one other worker will be on the other side standing here to milk the cows."

Evan asked, "So where's all this milk going to?"

"I'm getting there, don't worry." James said as he picked up a black hose with four suction tubes on the ends of it. He told Evan, "This is a milking machine. We have five of them on each side. You place it on the cows' teats, and it sucks all the milk out."

Evans' eyes widened as he began to picture it in his head.

James continued, "This machine's parts are all connected to each other and the milk travels down one tube. Follow me." James said as he began to walk out of the barn.

They walked into a smaller building where there was a huge tank right in the middle.

"This is where all the milk ends up." James said. "This refrigerator keeps the milk cold and stores it until the truck comes to pick it up every other day."

"Seems pretty simple." Evan said.

James grinned as he said to Evan, "Oh, this ain't even half of it. Let's walk back here."

They walked behind the barns and to a large shelter.

"This is where all the cows are held when they ain't in the fields. The biggest job of all is getting them all together and into the barn." James looked at his wristwatch and said, "Well, it's about that time. Let's get started."

Evan was trying hard to remember everything that James had told him in a short amount of time. James walked back over to the barn and came out with a shovel.

He handed it to Evan and said, "Here, you'll be needing this today."

Evan slowly took the shovel and asked, "For what?"

James gave him that grin again and replied, "Oh you'll see."

As the other men began to walk over, James told Evan, "Now for today, just think of this as a job shadow …but don't be afraid to use that shovel."

Evan stood by as he watched one of the men help line the cows up outside and take five cows in on each side. After several minutes, the cows would come out of the barn and a new set would go in. This process was repeated over and over as there were over one hundred cows to be milked. Evan saw that it was a lengthy process. It soon became obvious to him what the shovel was for as manure began to cover the ground of the holding area for the cows. He had never had to do much manual labor, but it was now his assignment. He was being humbled yet again. He laughed to himself as he thought of where he had once been and where he was now… scooping up cow crap. Still, he knew it was his choice to be here. Another choice that he couldn't question. To Evan, this was all new; but, after abandoning all of the many things he had once been involved in, he understood he better get the hang of it.

The sun was beginning to set as they finished up the afternoon's work. After hours spent shoveling manure and tossing around hay, Evan had no energy left.

As he was washing his hands at the sink in one of the barns, James walked up behind him and asked, "Want to give up yet?"

"Yes I do, but there's no way I'm going to." Evan said.

James patted him on the back and said, "Be ready at 4 a.m. It'll be just us two milking tomorrow."

James had tested Evan on his first day to see if he was really up to a job like this. Seeing Evan's determination made James feel more confident that the farm could continue to operate and that he could stay in the place he loved.

With an aching back, Evan slowly walked toward the house. He used the steps to wedge off his boots, and he went inside the house. He knew there was no chance that he'd go anywhere for the rest of the night. His stomach began to growl, so he looked in the refrigerator. There was a rotisserie chicken in a package. After double checking the expiration date, Evan heated it up and began to eat it alone in the quiet house. All of the sudden, he heard the turn of a key in the side door of the house, and James walked in with a bag of food.

"James? What are you doing?" Evan asked.

"Well, I've always come here to eat after working, why stop?" James said as he sat down across from Evan.

The next morning James again took Evan by surprise when he walked in the bedroom and flipped on the lights. He walked over beside the bed and grabbed Evan's shoulder.

Evan sat up in bed, looked at the clock, and said, "James? What are you doing? It's ten minutes until 4."

James replied, "Trust me, I know how you feel. I remember my first morning of work here. I didn't feel like going nowhere at four o'clock in the morning neither but right back asleep."

Every morning, Evan would ask himself *Is this really worth it?* As time went on, that question would answer itself when he saw and did things that changed his whole perspective … not only on life, but also on the people in his life. He soon built a bond with James that he could have never imagined having with anyone. After the early mornings of milking, they continued the tradition of eating fresh eggs and coffee at the same table where James and Linwood had sat every day for so many years.

After completing breakfast on the first morning on the job, Evan realized this new routine would prevent him from going anywhere for a while. Needing more of his belongings, he took the few hours of freedom he had during the day to go home. He knew his mother needed to know what was going on with him, and he felt he owed it to her to shed the light on the truth. The traffic was not bad, so it didn't take too long to get there. He felt much better when he drove back into the neighborhood than he had when he had left for his grandfather's funeral.

When he drove into the driveway, he saw his mother outside in her flower bed preparing for the spring season. She saw him coming and stopped what she was doing. When he got out of the car, she could tell there was something different about him. Evan had a big smile on his face like she hadn't seen in a long time.

She wrapped her arms around her son and asked, "Evan, what's going on?"

"That's what I came here to tell you." he said, "You won't believe it." Her face showed that she was eager to hear what he had to say. "My name was on my Grandfather Linwood's will." Evan said.

"All that land he had? That's great! No wonder you're happy … that's a lot of money." she said.

Evan replied, "Well, here's the part you won't believe … I'm keeping it all."

"But that farm … how will you ever begin to keep up with that?" she asked.

"It's not just me doing it, Mom." Evan said, "It sounds like you're not too crazy about this idea."

She replied, "I just want what's best for you, Evan."

"I do too. That's why I'm doing this." he said as he kissed her forehead and went inside to pack up a few things he would be needing for his new home.

Evan gave it his all on a daily basis to learn everything he could about this new job. Each day he felt closer to knowing who he truly was. He still wasn't accustomed to living in a farmhouse that felt so empty. It seemed as if faded memories filled the entire place, but the people who had made them were all gone. Evan walked up the stairs to the second floor and pulled down the ladder that led to the small attic above. He found the several bins filled with scrapbooks that Linwood had shown him and brought them all downstairs. Every chance he got, he would open the books and the memories came alive. He could only hope that many more wonderful memories would be made in that house,

Evan thought of those future memories as he looked forward to the end of each day after work was completed. Every night, he would lie on the guest room bed making a phone call to hear the voice of Mason. On every call he would hear something new from his son as he gave him an entire run down of what had happened that day. He continued to grow closer to Mason and Angela even though weeks had gone by since he had seen them. He desperately missed the afternoons with his son and wished there was something he could do to make things easier. Evan wasn't the only one who was missing that time. Angela had begun to truly realize what Evan meant to her. She was now convinced how different he was from the person she knew a few years ago. She was truly thankful that he was in Mason's life. That made her appreciate him more than ever.

Every evening when it was time for Mason to go to sleep, he'd tell Evan goodnight and hand his mother's phone back to her. Instead of hanging up the way she had done at first, Evan and Angela would have their own conversation. Angela had found herself confiding in Evan more and more. Now there were no awkward silences. They found lots to talk about. Usually the call ended with a simple "Goodnight." That night was different. Instead of simply saying *goodnight,* there was something Evan had been meaning to say for a while.

"Hey, Friday afternoon, you guys should come here after work." He suggested to her.

"I never thought you'd ask." she responded, "Just tell me where to go, and we'll be there."

Hearing her say that, Evan knew that no more time should be wasted. Evan couldn't get the two of them off his mind the rest of the week. The week seemed to go by slowly for Evan. On Friday as he and James finished up their morning work, they washed up and headed inside as they always did.

Just as James began to open the door, Evan asked, "Hey, is there any way I could finish up about an hour early this afternoon?"

James paused for a moment and asked, "Hour early? Why's that?"

"I invited my son and Angela up here. I haven't seen them in a few weeks, you know?" Evan replied.

James smiled and said nothing as he opened the door to the house. Evan followed him inside; but instead of stopping in the kitchen, he headed to the bedroom. He opened the drawer where he had put the ring box, took it out, and headed back to the kitchen.

Holding the opened box for James to see the ring, he said, "That will be okay, right?"

James, with eyes widening as he saw the ring, said, "Well then, right. That's all you had to say." He responded with a laugh.

Friday afternoon had finally come around, and Evan's adrenaline was on high as he anticipated Angela and Mason's arrival at the farm. The first couple of hours of the afternoon work felt as if it would never end. It was finally a few minutes before 6:00 when Evan nodded to James, pointing at his watch. As he left the barn, one of the other men stepped in his place. He hustled from the dairy barn and went into the house to clean up. Evan hurriedly showered and dressed. Then he scrambled around the closet to find his jacket with the ring in the pocket where he had put it. He put the jacket on and walked back to take one last look in the bathroom mirror. Just as he walked out on the porch, he saw Angela's car driving up the road toward the farm. He waved and walked toward the car as soon as it pulled into the driveway.

"I never thought we'd get here!" Angela said as she got out of the car.

Evan replied, "Believe me, I thought the same thing."

He walked over to the other side of the car and opened Mason's door. Mason jumped out of the car and into Evan's arms. He was so excited to see him for the first time in weeks.

"Why did you have to move?" Mason asked Evan.

"Mason! What did I tell you?" Angela said. Evan tried to laugh it off and changed the subject by saying, "Look, I've got a special place I want to take you guys. Follow me." he said. They walked together toward Linwood's pickup truck.

"Already? You don't want to show us around here first?" Angela asked.

Evan said, "You will have time to see what is here, trust me; but this comes first …

what I want to show you is well worth seeing.

The Question

Evan turned onto the long dirt road for the first time since he had been there with Linwood. The ride continued on to where the never-ending fields became visible. He looked over at Angela as she was looking out the window and taking it all in.

"I know what you're thinking" He said, "We're almost there, I promise."

When she looked over to smile at him, Evan knew he could stare in her eyes forever. They continued to the gate where he got out of the car to unlock it.

Mason asked, "Mommy, where are we?"

She replied, "I have no clue. Evan knows. That's all that matters."

The evening sun began to shine brighter through the windshield into their faces. Evan put down the sun visor as he drove toward the cabin. His heart was pounding at a rapid pace. He felt nervous knowing the time was nearing. He was thinking of nothing other than the fact that he knew the time for his next step was now. They reached the cabin and got out of the car. Evan's eyes fell on the two chairs that had been left from the special night he had with Linwood in front of the fire.

He snapped out of the reminiscent moment as Angela said, "This is a cute little place."

"Oh, yeah. I guess you could say that." he said as he stood back to get a good look at it. He continued, "Here, I don't think you want you to miss this."

He walked over and picked up the two chairs as Angela held Mason's hand

and led him into the cabin. The sun was beginning to set and the view through the porch screen was turning into a masterpiece. Angela settled into a chair on the porch and Evan placed the two chairs he had picked up beside her.

"Here, Mason. Take a seat." Evan said.

Mason sat down in one seat and Evan sat in the one beside it. Evans heart was so full. As he looked at Angela and Mason there in that setting, he saw a whole new masterpiece to which no sunset could compare.

Evan had turned the lanterns on inside the cabin as it began to grow darker. He knew that time wasn't on his side and he had something that he needed to say to Angela. Mason's attention was focused on a game he was playing on his tablet there on the porch. Now was the time.

Evan stood up from his seat and asked Angela in a quiet voice, "Hey, can you come with me for a minute?"

"Oh sure." she said as she stood up and walked with him into the room.

"That was beautiful … this was really a treat." she said.

"I just wish we had more time." he said.

"More time?" she asked, "What do you mean?"

Evan replied, "You know, it's different now. I just wish I could be there with you and Mason all of the time."

"We're just in two different places now." she said.

"But I want more than to hear your voices on the phone every day. I want the moments with you." Evan told her.

He knew it was time for the next step had to be taken. Evan began to put his hand in his coat pocket for the ring box when suddenly Mason looked back into the room and asked, "Are we gonna leave?"

Evan's eyes closed in disbelief. What seemed like the perfect moment had slipped away.

Angela had no idea what was in Evan's mind as she looked at him and said, "Well, it is getting late and we have to drive back home."

Evan tried to play it cool as he responded, "Well, that's a good point. Guess we can get going."

They walked out of the cabin into the dark night. Evan looked up in the sky and noticed all of the stars scattered in the sky and closed his eyes for a moment. He could just imagine himself walking away from a moment he wasn't sure he would ever get back.

The ride back to the farm house was silent. The only noise heard came from the truck tires on the gravel road. After arriving back at the farm, they got out of the truck and began to walk towards her car.

"We'll see you tomorrow." Angela said to Evan as they neared the car.

"Tomorrow?" Evan asked.

"You know, the first soccer practice." Angela reminded Evan.

Evan had completely forgotten, but still responded, "Oh yes, of course. I'll be there."

He said goodnight and waved to Mason who had been quiet for most of the night. Angela shut her car door and smiled through the window at Evan. He stood there and watched as she backed out of the driveway. He watched the taillights of her care as she drove away. He slowly turned and walked into the house, flipped on the lights, and took off his coat. He reached his hand in his pocket for the box. As he pulled it out, he opened it up and took a long look at the ring. After all this time, it was shining brighter than ever. He shoved the box back into his coat pocket feeling hopeless. Evan then walked into Linwood's bedroom, a room he didn't go into very often. He felt like there was still a boundary there he was crossing when he walked through the door … like he was invading a space that didn't belong to him. In this moment that boundary didn't matter at all. He had a need to go in there. He walked into the room and turned on the light. He walked straight over to the nightstand and picked up the old wedding picture beside the lamp. Holding it in his hands, he knew he had never wanted anything more than he wanted to marry Angela.

The next day, as soon as Evan finished his morning work, he quickly went inside to clean himself up. With no time for his usual breakfast, Evan decided to just stop somewhere. As soon as he walked out of the door, he saw James approaching the house.

"Where you headed?" James asked.

Evan replied, "I had completely forgot that I told Mason I would coach his soccer team."

James began to laugh, and he said, "A coach too? You do it all, I see. You try not to have too much fun out there."

Evan just couldn't help but laugh as he walked away and began the drive to the park. He arrived and drove into the parking lot that was completely filled with cars. He noticed each field had kids running around with one or two adults with them. As Evan walked closer to the field, he saw Angela sitting on the bleachers. She saw him about the same time; and, before he could say anything, she pointed out onto the field. He saw Mason and a group of other kids running around kicking a soccer ball. Evan jogged out to where they were and approached the man who was with them.

The man saw Evan coming and asked, "You Evan Stevenson?"

"Yeah, that's me" Evan replied.

"You're late." the man said with a straight face. "I got them started. Good luck." he told Evan as he walked away.

Evan stood back and didn't know where to begin. It seemed like uncontrollable kids were running everywhere. He then looked over at Angela and shook his head as she began to laugh.

Nearly an hour had gone by, but to Evan it felt like forever. It was spent trying to organize a group of kids to play a sport with which he wasn't that familiar. The only rule he knew was to kick the ball, and that's all he and Mason had ever done. After the kids huddled up around him to end practice, they each ran to their parents who were waiting for them. Mason stuck with Evan as he walked over to Angela. When Mason got closer to her, she bent down and gave him a hug.

"I'm so proud of you." she said.

She had never thought she would see the day her son would be part of any team. He had always been singled out his entire life until the day Evan had given him the support he desperately needed. Mason still had no idea who Evan truly was. All he knew was that he was his friend, and that's all he cared about.

Angela then looked at Evan and said, "And thank you, for everything."

"Oh don't worry about it." Evan said with a smile. "Hope to see you soon."

He held out his hand for Mason and said, "Good job today. You did great as always."

Mason smiled big and slapped Evan's hand with excitement.

Evan then turned around and headed for his car. When he got to it, he opened the back door and grabbed his coat to put it in the trunk. When he grabbed it, the small box fell from the pocket onto the ground. He was surprised to see it as he had forgotten that he had put it back in the coat pocket. He quickly picked it up and put it in his shorts pocket, He threw the coat in the trunk. He felt the box in his pocket and then turned to his left to see Angela holding Mason's hand as they walked toward where her car was parked in the parking lot. He had no prior plans to go anywhere else but back to the farm where he now called home. However, for some reason something entirely off his radar came to mind. There was something he hadn't remembered to do. When he thought of it, he began to feel better about how things had turned out the night before. He had completely skipped over the very important first step in making the commitment he needed to make. He quickly left the park and made his way over to the Sanders' household, where he needed to have a conversation with Mr. Sanders.

The sun was brightly shining on the late Saturday morning as Evan turned back onto Cypress Road. He drove to the end of the street and saw what he was hoping for. Mr. Sanders' large pickup truck was parked in the driveway. Evan parked on the side of the street. As he walked up the driveway toward the house, he noticed that Mr. Sanders was in his workshop repairing a lawn mower. He had turned around when he heard Evan's car door shut and stood up to see Evan walking toward him.

"Evan Stevenson, what another surprise. I see you don't have my daughter with you this time." he said with a look of disappointment.

"No sir, it's just me." Evan said.

Mr Sanders turned around and sat back down to continue his work.

"So, what brings you here?" he asked Evan.

"There's something I need to do, but asking you is the only way I'd be able to do so." Evan said.

Mr. Sanders had his back towards Evan as he continued to work, but he was listening to everything he said.

"Sir," Evan began to say before being interrupted by Angela's father.

"Son, I know where this is going." Mr. Sanders said as he stopped what he was doing and got himself together.

Evan hadn't been able to see the shocked look on Mr. Sanders face nor the tears beginning to build up in his eyes.

He continued, "The fact you've come here today to ask me anything regarding my daughter gives me all the answers I'd need to know."

Evan reached for the box in his pocket and opened it up, exposing the ring. He then placed it in front of Mr. Sanders for him to see. He picked it up and looked at it, then stood up and held his hand out for Evan to shake.

Before Evan left, all he could say was "Thank you."

Angela's father quickly responded, "Thank you, too. You've done more for us than you'll ever know."

Evan wasn't able to understand the impact he had made. All he could do was smile and accept his gratitude. As he walked out of the workshop into the warm day, he realized it was time to again ask Angela a very important question. This time he would be making a bigger commitment. He now just needed to create the perfect moment to do so.

As soon as Evan got into his car he reached for his phone and tried to call Angela. He anxiously waited for her to pick up, but it continued to ring. Finally, it went to her voicemail and Evan said into the phone, *"Hey it's Evan, just needed to ask something, well a few things actually. Anyway, call me back."* After putting his phone back into his pocket, he took a deep breath. He tried to calm himself down and relax as his hand were shaking on the steering wheel.

When Evan arrived back to the farm, he placed his phone on the counter and opened up the refrigerator to grab a horseshoe shaped sausage to cook. As he opened up the cabinet to pull out a frying pan, he heard his phone buzzing on the counter. He immediately reached for it. It was Angela calling him back.

He swiped his finger across the screen to answer and said, "Hey!"

"Hey, everything okay?" Angela asked.

"Oh yeah everything's great!" Evan enthusiastically replied.

"What was it that you needed to ask me?" Angela asked Evan.

"I just want to have a time where it will be just the two of us." Evan said.

"The two of us? Why's that?" Angela wondered aloud.

"There's a very important date that I wanted to schedule." Evan replied.

"Oh, I understand now." she said, thinking it had to do with Mason's birthday coming up.

"Well, when do you want to do it?"

"How about here, Friday evening. You can get that tour that you wanted yesterday." Evan said. "Okay, I guess that'll work." Angela said, even though she had not expected to go all the way back to the farm.

"Sounds good. I'll see you then." Evan said as he hung up the phone.

He stood there for a while after he placed the phone back onto the counter… and he yelled out loud to himself, *"This is really happening."*

Throughout the week, James assumed that Evan had already proposed. It wasn't until Friday morning while eating breakfast with Evan that he learned differently.

"I'll need to get off a little early from work this afternoon." Evan said.

James replied, "Look now, we can't make this an every Friday thing."

"I was hoping I wouldn't have to do this again, but things just didn't work out last week." Evan told him.

"How hard could it possibly be? You want me to do it for you?" James jokingly said.

"A lot harder than I thought it'd be." Evan replied.

As James grabbed his plate and stood up from his seat he told Evan, "All I can say is that you better walk in smiling tomorrow morning."

Evan grinned and replied, "I sure hope so."

As the afternoon's milking had gone on for a few hours, it was once again time for Evan to clock out. He turned around to James as it neared six o'clock and pointed to the door.

James gave him a thumbs up and loudly said, "Hey, this time just don't forget to ask."

After saying that, the other men in the barn began to laugh as James had informed them on what happened last week. Evan couldn't help but grin as he shook his head in embarrassment.

As soon as Angela got off work, she drove straight to the farm. Mason had been picked up from school by her parents and stayed there for the afternoon. In her everyday work attire and with her hair up as usual, it was just a normal day for Angela. She didn't have any idea what was about to happen. After Evan rushed to clean up, he felt more pressure this time than he did last week. He knew the rest of his life depended on how this night would go. He walked out of the house wearing jeans and a collared shirt. He stood by the door and looked at his watch. It was half past six o'clock. As soon as he took his eyes off the watch, he saw Angela's car coming toward the driveway. He felt his back pocket and realized he was missing the ring. Angela got out of her car walked toward Evan. He was undecided as to whether he should go greet her or run back inside to get the ring box.

As she got closer Evan waved with a smile and said, "Welcome back."

"After that car ride it makes being here even better." Angela said.

"So, I had an idea. Maybe we could go up to the lake again and talk there. Can't beat that view." Evan mentioned.

"Well, you are right about that. I guess we could do that." Angela said.

With relief, Evan responded, "Great, let me just run back in and get my sunglasses."

He walked back inside into the guest bedroom and took the ring box from his dresser. Before walking back out, he looked at Linwood's wedding picture again. Evan stuck the box in his sock not wanting it to be noticeable in his pocket. He then shut the door behind him and went to where Angela was waiting for him.

As they walked to the truck under the shelter, she asked, "You couldn't find them?"

"What's that?" Evan asked.

"Your sunglasses." Angela said.

"Oh right, of course. No I couldn't, I'll be just fine." Evan replied.

All during the ride over to the lake, Evan thought of the risk he was about to take. Recently he had been taking a lot of them. However, he knew that proposing to Angela would be the biggest one he could possibly take. Evan had found the missing piece which shed light onto so many other pieces that were left incomplete in his life. As he found those pieces, he grew to love them more than anything he had ever loved before. Risks had to be taken to find these things, and when he had found one it had led to another. There was still one more piece missing, and it was the biggest of them all. In order to put his life all together, he had to take the biggest risk that he had ever taken.

He drove quickly over the dirt roads leading up to the gate to make sure they'd catch a glimpse of the sun setting. After the entry wire was unlatched, he drove slower through the line of cherry trees. He noticed that each tree was in full bloom. Evan took it all in as it was one of the prettiest sights he could ever see, as Linwood had once told him. After he had parked the truck at the cabin, Evan got out and walked ahead of Angela. As he walked around the back of the cabin, he turned to Angela and said, "Follow me."

Before he began to walk down the steep stairs that led to the dock, he held out his hand for Angela. She stopped and looked at him and just couldn't help but smile. As they eased down the steps toward the dock, the lake was visible through the trees. When they got onto the dock, Angela stood still to take in the view. Evan carried two chairs stacked together. He unattached the one on top and put it in place for Angela to sit in. As she sat down, he bent down to feel the ring box that was in his right sock. With the two of them both seated, they both took in the calm and peace filled moment.

"This is absolutely wonderful." Angela said as she looked off into the distance. Evan quietly got up from his seat when he noticed that Angela was distracted by the view.

"So what was it you want to talk ab-" Angela started to ask as she turned to back toward Evan.

She wasn't able to finish her sentence as she was completely taken by surprise. Evan was down on one knee looking up at her. She put her hands over her mouth. She was not able to get another word out.

"I believe this belongs to you." Evan said as he began to open the box.

It was the ring she had once worn on her finger right there in front of her. She had thought she would never see again. She was completely speechless.

Evan was so emotional as he looked up in her eyes and said, "There has never been and never will be anyone like you. I've never stopped loving you, and I promise I never will. Will you let me fulfill that promise?"

Tears flowed down Angela's face as she nodded her head and said, "I thought you would never ask!"

With Evan smiling from ear-to-ear, he placed the ring on Angela's finger. He wrapped his arms around Angela while she sat there in awe. She felt the ring on her finger …

and leaned forward to receive Evan's kiss.

The New Image

They arrived back at the farm, but neither one of them wanted the evening to end. She knew she had to get back to her parents' home before too late to pick up Mason. They would be worried about her if she didn't. Evan took her hand in his and just sat there in silence for a moment. There was no way to describe how he felt, but he wanted to try. He looked toward Angela and saw the outline of her face in the moonlight. He had never seen anything more beautiful. He didn't know whether he was going to cry or smile … his emotions were all over the place. He knew he needed to say whatever he had to say because she would be leaving in a few minutes. He lifted her hand to his lips and kissed it softly.

"Angela" he said, "I don't deserve you after what happened so long ago; but I promise you I will make up for every minute we have missed together. I thought loved you then, but I didn't really know how to love anyone more than myself at that time. Now it is different, I have learned what true love is. I will love and cherish you and Mason as long as I live."

With that said, Angela made the first move for their first goodnight kiss.

They got out of the truck and walked hand in hand to her car. Evan embraced her again before she got in her car to drive back to town. He stood and watched as she baked out the driveway and turned out on the road. When the car lights were out of sight, he walked back inside into the house and straight to the bedroom where the wedding picture of his grandfather and grandmother sat on the table. He picked it, looked at it for a minute, then said out loud as if talking to his Grandfather Linwood, "Thank you. Thank you for showing me what love is all about." He sat the picture back on the table and he fell back onto the bed feeling like he was the happiest man alive.

Angela's heart was so full and so many thoughts from her past with Evan rushed through her mind. It seemed that all the bad memories had disappeared. She only remembered the fun times She thought about how Evan had just appeared out of nowhere in her front yard. Things like that only happened in fairy tales. It was as if he had been dead and had come back to life. She thought about the difference he had made in Mason's life. What more could she ask for?

In no time at all, she was back at her parents' house to pick up Mason. She sat in her car for a moment to gain her composure before going in. As she walked up to the door to knock, Mason opened it. Her mother was right beside him. They had heard the care drive up.

"Mason thought you would never come back," her mother said.

"I honestly felt the same way." Angela said, remembering how she had hated to leave Evan at the farm alone.

She had taken the ring off of her finger before getting out of the car, wanting to explain everything to her parents in private. Her father walked over from the living room and looked at her hand to see if there was a ring. Not seeing it, he thought. *"When on earth is that boy gonna ask her."* After a few words, they all walked out with Angela as she and Mason were going to the car. They had conversation was about the soccer game the next morning. Angela opened the back door and helped Mason get fastened in his seat. She closed the door so Mason wouldn't hear what she was going to tell her parents. She wanted to tell him in private.

Facing her parents, Angela reached in her pocket and said, "Oh, and there was one more thing I need to mention."

She took the ring from her pocket and put it back on her finger and held her hand up for them to see. Her mother took a deep gasp of surprise. Mr. Sanders had not told his wife about Evan's visit and the permission he had granted. He knew she was never one to keep a secret. They both immediately held their arms out to hug her, knowing better than anyone how much she had been through. It had been a long, bumpy road since she had last had that ring on her finger. The missing pieces were now coming together. Her parents stood there together with happy looks on their faces and watched as she backed out of the driveway. Their relationship with their only child had been restored, and the worries about their grandson been relieved. Evan Stevenson, of all people, was the one to thank.

The next morning back at the farm, James didn't even have to ask how the night before went. As soon as Evan walked in the dairy barn, James was met with the biggest smile he'd ever seen. Evan wore that same smile throughout the entire day. After working, Evan made the drive to the park to coach Mason's soccer team. As usual, he arrived a few minutes late and at the same time Angela did. Her parents were there waiting and couldn't help but notice the three of them walking toward the fields together. The happiness that each of them felt was very obvious. That happiness was something that each of them very much deserved.

The game had started and Evan stood there in front of the bleachers watching his team. It was then that he realized where he was and what he was doing. It was at that moment that he knew there wasn't anywhere else he'd rather be. With his team huddles and high fives and laughs, Mason had finally felt as if he belonged somewhere. He was now a part of something greater than he could've ever imagined. Again, Evan Stevenson was the one to thank.

After the game was finally over, Evan hoisted Mason up on his shoulders as they walked off of the field.

When they got to the parking lot, Evan placed Mason back on his feet and asked, "Y'all want some lunch?"

Mason jumped in the air with excitement and Angela replied, "Well, there's your answer."

They got into Evan's car and after getting a few minutes down the road, Evan asked Angela, "You mind if we make a detour? There's something I need to do."

Angela replied, "Yeah. I guess that's okay."

She wasn't quite sure where they were going; but, as they continued to drive, she recognized the area. Past the busy section of the city and into the suburbs, they then turned into a place where she hadn't been in years. Angela knew now exactly where she was as they passed the huge brick houses with long driveways. They then turned into the driveway that circled around the front yard.

Evan looked at Angela and said, "When I look at the car, you and Mason come on out of the car."

Angela nervously replied, "Are you sure about this."

"Positive." Evan said as he opened the door.

Angela watched as Evan slowly walked behind the car and to the door. He reached for his keys that he usually took everywhere he went. His empty pocket reminded him that he didn't have his keys with him. He then pressed the doorbell and took a step back. After a few seconds, the door opened and his mother stood there in front of him.

"Evan, it's you." she said as she reached her arms out to hug him.

"Hey, Mom. You looking amazing as always." Evan said.

She smiled and then said, "Well come on in, dear."

"Well, we have to talk." Evan told her.

"Okay, sure." she said as she noticed the car parked in the driveway.

"Who's car is that?" She asked.

Evan grabbed her hand and said, "Life has moved really fast over the past months. I haven't done a good job of including you in a lot of it, and I'm sorry for that."

"Oh don't worry about that." His mother insisted.

Evan continued, "I know I haven't been open about all the changes in my life, but now I want them all to be seen."

He then turned around to look at the car. Angela, who had been watching the entire conversation, saw Evan turn around. She took a deep breath and opened her car door. As she got out of the car, the first thing his mother noticed was her blonde hair. In that moment she realized what was going on. Still, there was no way to begin to prepare her for what was next. Without looking up, Angela opened the back door and lifted Mason from his car seat. Still wearing his soccer uniform, he held his mother's hand as they walked towards Evan.

Evan's mother took a step back as she placed her hand over her mouth in disbelief.

She began to say, "Is that..."

"Yes." Evan replied, "It's who you think it is."

She looked at the young boy and saw a replica of her son at that age. As Angela lifted her head, his mother instantly recognized her like she hadn't changed a bit. Evan let go of his mother's hand and walked down the step. He held his arm out to Angela and looked up at his mother.

Evan said, "Mom, I want to introduce you to my family." She stood still and looked down noticing the ring on Angela's finger. As she looked at the three of them, she became emotional. Tears welled up in her eyes, but at the same time a smile spread across her face.

All of a sudden a voice came from inside the house. As soon as Evan heard it, he knew that the joyous moment would immediately end.

"What on earth is going on? Why's the door wide open?" the voice said.

Evan's mother stood back and his grandfather appeared in the doorway. He walked out and saw Evan standing there... but his grandson was not alone. He saw standing beside Evan a beautiful young woman whose face he knew. He recognized her as the girl he had constantly urged his grandson to stop chasing years ago. Beside the woman stood a young boy ... a young boy who looked exactly the way he remembered Evan looking what seemed like such a short time ago. He stood there in complete silence for what seemed like a lifetime. His past rolled before his very eyes and he saw himself as a young man again ... a young man with a beautiful wife and a daughter. That daughter had brought Evan into his life. Without a father being there for Evan, he had assumed the role of being his guardian and grandfather. His mind was filled with thoughts of both his past and the present. In that moment, he realized how the expectations he had of his grandson were so different from the life Evan really wanted. He knew that time was not on his side. He needed more years than he had left to make up for all the pain and frustration that he had caused.

It took him a moment to gather his composure. In the past few months, he had known that Evan's mind was consumed with something bigger than his career, but he had no idea what was really happening in his life. He now realized he had been trying to keep Evan from what mattered most to him. It was like a bolt of lightning had hit him when he thought of what he had done. He felt lower than he ever had. His pride completely faded away.

Evan saw the confused look on his grandfather's face.

He started to walk toward him and said, "Look…"

Before he could say more, his grandfather shook his head and eased closer to Evan. A single tear rolled down his face as he stood there and looked into Evan's eyes. Without shame, he opened his arms wide and embraced his grandson and began to weep. He let out all of the years of guilt and shame. Evan was totally shocked, and his emotions teeter-tottered as he reached out his arms and wrapped them around his grandfather. This was the same man who had always been impossible to please. Evan didn't know what to think of what was happening. What he did know was that he should accept his embrace. After a minute or so the man who had never hugged Evan before released him and took a step back.

He wiped his eyes and said, "Well, please come on in."

As his mother watched from the doorway, she became even more emotional. The difficult and confusing past several months began to make perfect sense, and her father finally seemed to understand that Evan had to be his own man. They all walked together through the front door of the house into the den where they spent time filled with conversation and years' worth of catching up. Grandfather, by spending this time with his great grandson, Mason, knew that his legacy would live on.

What Evan had thought would be a pop-in visit with his mother had turned into a life-changing event. He had no idea something like this would happen. He wished they could stay longer, but he needed to go with Angela and Mason. They had quite a distance to travel to their new home at Linwood Johnson's farm. They said their goodbyes and were now anticipating the next visit together. As they made their way out of the house and down the steps to the car, his mother and grandfather stood and watched the three of them walk away.

As Evan walked back to the car behind Angela and Mason, he felt like everything was in slow motion. He was so glad they had taken the time to make this visit. After getting Angela and Mason in the car, he paused to reach in his pocket for his wallet. Out of it he pulled the picture that was taped together. After this visit and because of that picture, there were no more questions looming over him. The unimportant things that had once motivated him in life were no longer a part of who he was. What he had found would last forever. He no longer had to close his eyes to live his dream; he was now living it. Every future moment's good memories would be made together with the two people right there with him ...

memories as far as the eye can see.

Made in the USA
Columbia, SC
14 June 2021